NECROSCOPE®

HARRY
AND
THE PIRATES

TOR BOOKS BY BRIAN LUMLEY

THE NECROSCOPE® SERIES

Necroscope

Necroscope II: Vamphyri!

Necroscope III: The Source

Necroscope IV: Deadspeak

Necroscope V: Deadspawn

Blood Brothers

The Last Aerie

Bloodwars

Necroscope: The Lost Years

Necroscope: Resurgence

Necroscope: Invaders

Necroscope: Defilers

Necroscope: Avengers

Necroscope: Harry and the Pirates and Other Tales from the Lost Years

TALES OF THE PRIMAL LAND

The House of the Cthulhu

Tarra Khash: Hrossak!

Sorcery in Shad

THE TITUS CROW SERIES

Titus Crow, Volume One: The Burrowers Beneath & The Transition of Titus Crow

Titus Crow, Volume Two: The Clock of Dreams & Spawn of the Winds

Titus Crow, Volume Three: In the Moons of Borea & Elysia

THE PSYCHOMECH TRILOGY

Psychomech

Psychosphere

Psychamok

OTHER NOVELS

Demogorgon

The House of Doors

Maze of Worlds

Khai of Khem

SHORT STORY COLLECTIONS

Fruiting Bodies and Other Fungi

The Whisperer and Other Voices

Beneath the Moors and Darker Places

Harry Keogh: Necroscope and Other Weird Heroes!

NECROSCOPE®

HARRY AND THE PIRATES

AND OTHER TALES FROM THE LOST YEARS

BRIAN LUMLEY

TOR®

A TOM DOHERTY ASSOCIATES BOOK
NEW YORK

NECROSCOPE®: HARRY AND THE PIRATES

Copyright © 2009 by Brian Lumley

A Tor Book
Published by Tom Doherty Associates, LLC
175 Fifth Avenue
New York, NY 10010

www.tor-forge.com

Tor® is a registered trademark of Tom Doherty Associates, LLC.

Library of Congress Cataloging-in-Publication Data

Lumley, Brian.
    Necroscope. Harry and the pirates and other tales from the lost years / Brian Lumley.
        p. cm.
    "A Tom Doherty Associates book."
    ISBN-13: 978-0-7653-2338-5
    ISBN-10: 0-7653-2338-9
    I. Title. II. Title: Harry and the pirates and other tales from the lost years.
    PR6062.U45N45 2009
    823'.914—dc22

                                                                2009012920

First Edition: July 2009

Printed in the United States of America

0 9 8 7 6 5 4 3 2 1

For
Dave the Web,
Keith and Sarah,
Sharon and Joanne,
John, and Paul, and
all the rest of
the KeoghCon
Gang

Contents

Introducing Harry Keogh: Necroscope   9

For the Dead Travel Slowly   13

Harry and the Pirates   111

End Piece: Old Man with a Blade   186

Introducing Harry Keogh: Necroscope

On the opening page of the first 1986 British edition of *Necroscope*—the page I have always called the "blurb page," where a juicy, or action-packed, or especially gripping paragraph has been taken from the text and reprinted as a hook for the potential reader, that fellow browsing in the bookstore—I cajoled my publisher to feature a concoction, found nowhere else in the book, which then and now I considered not only a fair description of what a Necroscope is, but also one "grabber" of a blurb. It goes like this:

DEFINITIONS:

Tele- (Gk. *tele:* "far")

   A telescope is an optical instrument which enlarges the images of distant objects. Example: the surface of the moon may be viewed as from a few hundred miles away.

Micro- (Gk. *mikros:* "small")

   A microscope is an optical instrument which makes even tiny objects visible to the human eye. Under a microscope a drop of clear water is seen to contain myriad unsuspected micro-organisms.

Necro- (Gk. *nekros:* "a corpse")

   A Necroscope is a human instrument with access to the minds of the dead. Harry Keogh is the Necroscope— he knows the thoughts of corpses in their graves.

9

The main differences between these instruments is this—the first two perform purely physical, one-way functions and are incapable of changing anything: the moon cannot look back through the telescope; the amoeba does not know it is under microscopic scrutiny.

That's Harry Keogh's big problem: his talent seems to work both ways. **THE DEAD KNOW—AND THEY WON'T LIE STILL FOR IT!**

Well, that was my "blurb," my hook some twenty-two years ago, and I'm still happy with it despite that it doesn't paint the whole or even the true picture. Instead it makes it appear that the teeming dead are out for revenge! Which in the Necroscope's case could scarcely be further from the truth; for the dead love him! (Well, let's put it this way: the "Great Majority" of them love him.)

But between the living and the dead there are the undead, and that's another story. In fact it's a story that has taken most of the last two decades to write, a period covering seven bulky novels and a book of shorter stories, plus a stand-alone novel and two trilogies in which Harry Keogh plays cameo roles in the exploits of several new and very different Necroscopes.

As for the original Necroscope:

The man—and sometimes his avatar or reincarnation—has faced all kinds of mankind's enemies: spies, vampires, zombies, werewolves, and aliens, often recruiting such to a cause which has cost Harry his life more than once! But . . . does that mean that he is dead? Or even doubly dead? No, for now as then he's out there somewhere. . . .

Fiction has given us a whole host of Harrys. There's been Harry Lime, as played by Orson Welles, Dirty Harry Callahan, as played by Clint Eastwood, and a certain amount of "Trouble With Harry" too! There's been superspy Harry Palmer, played by Michael Caine; but most recently and notably there's been the phenomenally successful Harry Potter and his marvellous adventures at Hog-warts school for magicians, in the bestselling books and smash-hit movies that have left every other modern fiction novelist floun-dering, if not washed up, in J. K. Rowling's wake.

Myself, I'm delighted with Harry Potter! Not only has he en-tertained millions the world over—young people mainly, for whom he was designed, but adults also—Harry has introduced many of them for the first time to the weird, wonderful worlds of fantasy fiction. And as everyone knows, children grow up and tastes change. Right now they are obsessed with this young man, with *their* Harry, and rightly so. But tomorrow and tomorrow?

Well, while the future is a devious thing, I think it only fair to say there's a darker Harry out there and far more adult magicks waiting. Already, and ever more frequently, I'm getting letters from young readers whose elders have introduced them to *my* Harry, to Harry Keogh, Necroscope.

And so, as the end of my writing career draws ever closer, and while I know I'll never catch up with J.K.R., still I'm far from floundering in her wake and very happy for the future. You see, I'm waiting a few more years for Harry Potter's readers to grow up. . . .

Here in this latest volume, the sixteenth, you'll find two long novellas and a—what, a vignette? An end piece, anyway—featuring the Necroscope in that period of his life previously designated "The Lost Years." And for those who may be interested, if for no other reason, I'll here append a complete listing of Necroscope titles and the dates when they were written, hopefully for your aproval.

Necroscope	March–September 1984
Necroscope II: Vamphyri!	February–August 1986
Necroscope III: The Source	April–August 1987
Necroscope IV: Deadspeak	November 1988–March 1989
Necroscope V: Deadspawn	March 1989–March 1990

Blood Brothers	May 1990–April 1991
The Last Aerie	June 1991–July 1992
Bloodwars	August 1992–August 1993
Necroscope: The Lost Years	January 1994–March 1995
Necroscope: Resurgence	May 1995–March 1996
Necroscope: Invaders	June 1997–June 1998
Necroscope: Defilers	June 1998–June 1999
Necroscope: Avengers	June 1999–June 2000
Harry Keogh: Necroscope and Other Weird Heroes!	June–August 2002
Necroscope: The Touch	November 2003–November 2004
Harry and the Pirates	January–July 2007

BRIAN LUMLEY
Torquay, August 2007

For the Dead Travel Slowly

In the gloom of the woods *something stirred, moving slowly and yet, for a Thing of its nature, paradoxically quickly and with purpose. It was an ancient Thing, and these woods had been its habitat for millennia. Upon a time centuries ago, a handful of its long-lived kind had dwelled in these selfsame woods, until all but this one had died in a vengeful fire.*

The last of its species, the Thing was as weird as can be, but then again the sweet rains and dark plasms of earth—and on occasion the salty juices and nutrients of other than clay-cold soil—have nurtured myriad bizarre species on the three-billion-year-old paths of evolution; while fires, usually but not always natural, have destroyed a great many more.

The Thing had intelligence that was more instinct; it was "sentient" in ways totally alien to men; it had nothing in the form of true emotions, except perhaps the frustration of loneliness and—in times of necessity, and others of ungovernable urges, when it sought out and fed lustfully upon certain alternatives to the bland *nutrients of soil and leaf-mould—something of the awful pleasure derived from indulging its needs.*

Being a survivor and asexual both, the Thing had recently become aware of an important fact: that after these many centuries it would soon be time to repro-duce, when bare subsistence on the mainly inert juices and minerals of earth would be insufficient to its needs. But it was summer, and summer had brought creatures into the borders of the forest; not little creatures like the ones that rustled in the fallen leaves or sang in the wood's highest branches and nested there, but other, larger beings who sought out secret, shady places in which to embrace.

Sexual activity . . . not that the old Thing understood very much about that, but it did understand the fatigue, the temporary loss of consciousness that often resulted from this behaviour; understood, welcomed, and even possessed a means of inducing such weariness. For in dimly remembered times past, through myr-iad summer seasons since, when lovers embraced in secrecy in these dark, uncut woods, then it had been *the old Thing's time.*

. . . And would be again!

It happened during the lost years, that chaotic, long-drawn-out period in the Necroscope Harry Keogh's life of which, later, he would "believe" he remembered much while in fact recalling noth-ing of any real substance, clarity, or durability. And while he would know he had employed a mathematical (indeed metaphysical) for-mula, unique in himself, to conjure a means of teleportation and en-able an exhaustive worldwide search for his runaway wife and infant son, still he would never manage to focus his memory upon more than a handful of the locations which he'd supposedly visited in this way. Vague and shifting landscapes, like forgotten phrases on the tip of his tongue, would form wraithlike yet frustratingly fa-miliar scenes in the dimmest corners of Harry's mind, collapsing into smoke there if he should attempt to bring them into perma-nence. Which was why—whenever he was caused to reflect on that persistently opaque period—thoughts that were usually inadvertent, or if not that then certainly reluctant—it would always be in terms of time lost. Even of *years* lost.

The lost years, yes . . .

All of this, however, this hiatus created by some blockage in Harry's mind, was just as well; and because deep in the core of his being he knew or suspected this was so, he took care not to pursue the mystery too closely. Certainly the macabre events of the years in question were not such as to invite examination or investigation by *any* entirely normal man—a statement which should *not* be construed to imply that Harry was entirely normal or natural. No, hardly that. Human and physically normal, certainly, but mentally, intellectually?—never! He was apart from other living men as they are apart from the Great Majority, the teeming dead. For despite that Harry Keogh was very much alive, as the Necroscope he was *by no means* apart from the dead!

"Necroscope": a composite word created by Harry Keogh himself, and the only word that accurately described him or rather his function. For as the *tele*scope spies on things afar and the *micro*scope scans the incredibly small, so a *Necro*scope tunes in on the thoughts of the dead and can even converse with corpses! But no faker Harry Keogh; no cheating, so-called "spiritualist" but the real thing, the world's only true master of matroclinic abilities passed down from genuine psychics: forebears of great power whose parapsychological talents had been inherited by one in whom even weirder skills, if such may be imagined, had evolved and continued to evolve if not entirely "naturally."

It was during those oh-so-confusing lost years, then—at a time when Harry had left his lonely old house near Edinburgh and returned to the fields, villages, and country lanes of the County of Durham on England's sadly declining north-east coast, that same region where he had grown to manhood, courted Brenda, and first explored his eerie skills—that the following incidents occurred. For it was in just such familiar settings, where yet again he had failed to discover a single clue to the whereabouts of his wife and infant son, that the Necroscope stumbled across something entirely different. . . .

It was summertime, and Harry was feeling tired, or not so much tired as drowsy; the heat of the summer sun was getting to him, and his face, his forearms, and his chest in the V of an open-necked shirt, were tanned to a degree that was unusual for him. Even a light tan would make a sharp contrast with the normally pallid complexion of one who was not by nature a sun worshipper. What, Harry Keogh, a sun worshipper? No, far more likely a child of the night, the Necroscope: a creature of the moon and stars, a familiar of cobwebs, shadows, and gloom . . . even of the gloomiest places of all, though the latter was more a matter of convenience than preference. For there in the darkness of the last and longest night, that was where the majority—even the Great Majority—of Harry's friends existed still.

It had not always been that way. In earlier, less troubled or problematic times when he was with his wife, things had been very different. Brenda had loved beaches, breezes off the sea, cliff-hugging paths and leaf-dappled forest ways; she'd enjoyed the grass-tufted sand-dunes at Crimdon Dene, the sprawling mile of pure white sand at Seaton Carew, the penny arcades and fish-and-chip shops of the seaside resorts. Which was why the Necroscope had done it all over again—the beaches, breezes, penny arcades, fish-'n'-chips, the lot—while he searched for Brenda. Which was also how he had earned the patch of mild but irritating sunburn on the crown of his head.

Today, having learned his lesson, Harry had worn a floppy, wide-brimmed hat that in its way looked camp on his young head; more especially so in the raw-knuckled ex-coal-mining village on the coast where he was staying, where the miner's flat grey cap was still the customary mode of headgear; this despite the fact that the local coal mines had closed down many years ago. For however much the fortunes of villages like Easingham, Blackhill

Rocks, Morton, and Harden had suffered with the decline of "the pits," somehow they managed to retain the character and customs of their salt-of-the-earth inhabitants; customs that would live on for some time yet, even as long as the last of the old-timers who had once hewed coal in the mines. But Harry's hat—however out of place it might look—had served a double, even a triple purpose. It kept the sun from his itching scalp (kept it out of his eyes, too) and, in the privacy of its floppy brim, he could mumble—*apparently* to himself—without being observed by anyone who might otherwise have reason to consider him an idiot.

At the moment, however—relaxing as best a restless nature would allow, in a deck chair, in the seclusion of the garden of a friend he had known since pre-teen secondary-modern school-days prior to the start of his technical education and the continuation of pursuits that were rather more esoteric—there was no fear of that.

His boyhood friend was James "Jimmy" Collins, who was once Captain of the school's football team and later became the best striker Harden Colliery Football Club ever had—until, at only seventeen years of age, his right knee bent sideways in a game and failed to get better, ever. Since when he had been an electrician like his father before him, which was a lot better than working down in the pits would have been, if they'd lasted longer. Despite Jimmy's alleged boyhood aversion to girls (he had once sworn that he would "hang himself from a goalpost" rather than get caught with his arm around a girl when the lights went up at the local cinema), he had ended up getting one in trouble, done the right thing and married her, and just seven months later learned that the baby wasn't his. No, it belonged to the youth he caught his wife with when he came home early from a job one morning. Well, he was not the first young man who had fallen for that one, and he certainly wouldn't be the last. Fortunately the little house his parents had given him as a wedding present was in his name; the "lady" had moved out—and right out of the district, too—and Jimmy had gone back to swearing off girls.

"Still weird, eh Harry?" Jimmy's voice broke the garden's sunny afternoon silence, and broke into Harry's mental privacy. Actually, it roused him from a drowsy, very-nearly-asleep condition of semi-consciousness. He'd been dreaming about . . . someone calling? A cry for help? A distant, desperate, and possibly dead voice? An SOS from beyond? Well, perhaps. But far more likely a daydream, gone now into that limbo where all dreams are said to have origin. Whichever, he wasn't too concerned; he had "heard" or become aware or conscious of several ill-defined, out-of-the-ordinary sounds or thoughts just recently, especially that time when he'd discovered that even fossils from Earth's prehistoric past can have "voices" of a sort.

Lifting his head, Harry blinked owlishly as Jimmy Collins came from the house into the garden. Jimmy was carrying chilled fruit drinks in tall glasses, one in each hand, and as he drew closer Harry muttered, "Eh? What's that you say?"

Jimmy nodded, and answered: "Yep, you're still weird! Even if I didn't recognize the physical Harry Keogh—or rather your face, which I couldn't, and didn't—still I think I would have sensed the weirdness anyway and known it was you. Like who else *could* it be, knowing what you knew? And you know something? For all that you look different, still the longer you're around and the more I see of you—even though you've only been here for a week—damned if you haven't started to look more and more like . . . well, like *you*! Like Harry! I mean like the Harry you used to be! *Damn!*"

Wide awake now, Harry knew precisely what the other meant. But grinning at his young old friend from the shade of his hat, and reaching for the welcome drink that Jimmy was offering him, still he said, "Oh yes? And after a muddled mouthful like that, you still have the nerve to call *me* weird? Was that English you were speaking just then, Jimmy?"

"*Huh!*" said his friend, pulling a face. "Oh, you're weird all right, Harry! But hey—is it any wonder I get my words all tangled? I mean, after all this time, showing up here, like . . . like *this*? Who else would have believed that story you told me, if not someone who would recognise Harry Keogh's weirdness, eh? It may have been a long time, but yours is a brand of peculiar that's unmistakable. Well to me it is, anyway."

"Precisely why I came to see you!" said Harry, with a curt nod. "Because I knew you would know it was me. But also to find out if you'd heard anything of Brenda; and to check on you, see how you were doing—because I'd heard you had problems. Yes, I knew you'd accept me, Jimmy . . . and you're right, it has been a long time since I moved from school here in Harden to the technical college in Hartlepool. After that, I don't know, we just seemed to lose touch."

Nodding, Jimmy seated himself in a deck chair next to the Necroscope. "Yes, we did," he said, "until you showed up again and asked me to be your Best Man. You and Brenda Cowell, sweethearts at first sight, or as nearly so as makes no difference." Reaching out, he lifted the floppy brim of Harry's hat to stare deep into the other's eyes, and continued: "Both of us married, eh, Harry? As it happens, way too young, and both regretting it. Mine has gone—good riddance, I say—and yours has flown the coop, leaving you to wonder why and to grieve over it."

"No," said Harry, "I don't think I am grieving any longer. And I *do* know why; at least I think I do. It's this new face of mine. My face, and my . . . my . . ." He paused for a single moment, then hurriedly went on: "And anyway, Jimmy, as you just pointed out, we were much too young. . . ." He had caught himself barely in time, having almost said, "my face *and body!*" Which could only have led to a lot more questions.

For the body he was wearing—despite that it was a good, healthy one—wasn't the original that he had been born inside. Neither the face, nor the body. No, for not long ago the Necroscope had undergone an astonishing, involuntary metempsychosis, until now "he," the mind and soul of Harry Keogh, inhabited the body of someone else. Mercifully that someone had been completely brain-dead when Harry commandeered his empty shell; there'd been no arguing over possession, as it were. But there had also been precious little hope that his wife would accept him in his new identity, and it was one of a number of reasons why she had fled and taken the baby with her; or more properly why the baby had caused or enabled her flight . . . which is another, and perhaps even stranger story . . . .

As if reading Harry's mind, Jimmy was now frowning, examinining his guest more closely and biting his lip as his narrowed eyes swept the Necroscope up and down. And finally, shaking his head, he said, "Even now—I mean, you *know* what I mean—even now I'm not quite, not entirely—"

"What, not sure, Jimmy?" Harry cut him short. "And is this the same bloke who stood beside me on the beach after I knocked that bully Stanley Green on his fat backside? Oh, you were sure enough then! There was a whole bunch of our classmates there. I had given Green a beating, then offered the same to anyone else who fancied it. I told them: 'What I said to this shit goes for the rest of you.' Something like that, anyway. Then I said: 'Or should any *one* of you just happen to fancy his chances here and now . . . ?' Which was when—"

"—When I came to stand beside you," Jimmy took over from him, "and said, 'Or any *two* of you?' There were no takers. *Huh!* They weren't cowards, just a bunch of ordinary school-kids. And after they'd seen big bully Green knocked down in the dirt, his nose all wobbly, blubbing and grovelling, they were relieved it was over, that's all. . . ."

Harry nodded. "Yes, that's exactly how it was. So then, is this me or isn't it?"

"Well, it better be," the other grinned ruefully. "Especially since you've been sleeping in my spare bedroom for a week! But even so you tell a damn strange story. Like, you were working for the government on a secret job when you were caught in an explosion that wrecked your face, so they fixed you up with plastic surgery? I mean, how weird is that?"

The Necroscope shrugged. He wasn't much for lying—certainly not to a friend—but he knew that the truth was stranger yet. Jimmy *really* wouldn't have been able to accept the truth, which would have thrown everything else into doubt, causing all sorts of complications. Harry might have had to find other lodgings, for one thing, or go back along the Möbius route to his place on the outskirts of Edinburgh every night, which wasn't a good idea. He was actually enjoying his time away from that old house, in the company of one of his few *living* friends from his school days, and the trouble with indiscriminate and unnecessary use of the Möbius Continuum was that he might be observed stepping out of nowhere when he arrived back in Harden one morning. Life was difficult enough already, and Harry was an adherent of the creed that the easiest plan is usually the best.

"I mean," Jimmy went on in that questioning manner of his, "why couldn't these secret government people fix you up with a younger face? Er, not that you're ugly, you understand, but was that the best they could do for you?"

Fortunately Harry had seen fit to devise an answer to that one in advance. "They couldn't just pick and choose, Jimmy!" he said. "And neither could I. This is how it came out, and that's it. And anyway, it serves a purpose: with these new looks I can go on working undercover, you know?"

Jimmy scratched his head. "My old pal has become some kind of secret agent!" he said. "Harry Keogh, aka 008! So why aren't you working 'undercover' right now—or are you? What, here in Harden? Hell no! No way! Impossible!—unless some crazed terrorist is building a nuclear device in one of Harden's old mineshafts! Mind you, he'd have to be *really* crazy, because there's not too much that's worth blowing to smithereens around here!"

"Ha! Ha!" said Harry, however humourlessly. "No, you know I'm looking for Brenda. See, I'm still a bit, er, shell-shocked after the explosion—just one of the hazards of being a field operative—and this is how I'm using some of my R and R time." He tried not to look or feel too guilty, and knew that in fact he *wasn't* guilty; for despite that he was lying now, it wasn't long ago that the Necroscope *had* been involved—in his unique way, and however involuntarily—in some vastly important work on behalf of a special branch of Her Majesty's Secret Services.

Now Jimmy sighed, shook his head, and said, "I still can't tell whether you're serious or not! But you're weird and that's for sure! What was it you were muttering to yourself when I was coming out of the house? You were asleep, or almost asleep. You were very still and quiet and seemed to be holding your breath, as if you were straining to hear someone or something. Then you began to mumble to yourself and I think I heard you say, 'What? Who? Where?' Something questioning like that, anyway. Now what was that all about? A nightmare maybe? Or rather, a daymare?"

Harry shrugged, and answered: "A bad dream? I suppose it's possible." And after sipping thoughtfully at his drink, he continued: "In which case maybe I should be grateful that you woke me up, eh? But whatever it was—and since I can't remember anything about it, it couldn't have been too important. No, it was just a common—'or garden'—dream, that's all. No big deal."

And perhaps it really wasn't such a big deal; but now that Jimmy had started him thinking about it—wondering why he'd seemed to be, what, "straining to hear someone or something?"— suddenly Harry wasn't nearly so sure about that. . . .

The fact was that the Necroscope *had* been hearing—or rather, sensing—things for some time now. The talent he had inherited from his female forebears (a talent which some, including Harry himself, might from time to time more readily consider a curse) was gradually becoming more acute in him. If it had been purely physical, as in diseased, malfunctioning hearing, then it might be diagnosed as tinnitus or a similar disorder. But how to diagnose a *meta*physical—indeed a parapsychological—condition as grotesque as this one, involving things which Harry "heard" not with his ears but with his mind? In a future as yet unimagined and unimaginable, he would name his dubious talent "deadspeak" when using it to communicate with deceased *people*. As for what he was experiencing now, however—

—While some of the things that "spoke" to or "informed" him were most definitely dead, they were *not* always people. . . .

In addition to which, there were perfectly normal mechanical sounds which Harry heard, naturally enough, with his ears. Out in the privacy of Jimmy's walled garden, for instance, the buzzing of bees in the roses and flower borders wasn't the only sound; there was also the infrequent drone of an airplane from on high, the sound of traffic from the main coast road, even the near-distant *clicketty-clack* of steel wheels on rails, wafting on the balmy summer air right across the sleepy village from Harden's old railway viaduct.

Of course, these were sounds that Harry heard like so much white noise—sounds he expected to hear—which in no way registered as other than ordinary. . . .

In that selfsame garden, however, beneath the overhang of inward-sloping terra-cotta tiles where they decorated the top of the high wall, several spiders had their webs, all more or less evenly spaced out so as to avoid territorial disputes. In those web larders of the spiders, the tiny corpses of flying—or at least once-flying—insects were neatly cocooned and hung like game to ripen. If Harry were to concentrate on these small dead creatures he would actually—and *had* actually—become conscious of a certain sensation, awareness or intuition: the merest glimmer, as faint in his unique mind as the fantasised sound of a snowflake's fall to earth might be in his ears. He had traced this *un*-sound to the fly mummies under the tiles.

And yet this was more than mere intuition, for Harry sensed the surprise, bewilderment, even the *indignation* of the drained midges. It was in a way "sentience"—according to that word's definition, at least—if not as men would normally understand and accept it. But in his mind it registered as a question—or more properly an infinitely small "why?"—to which there could never be any answer that the insects framing the question would understand.

They only understood that the freedoms they had known were no more, that their aerial scavenging and pheromone-driven contact with others of their species—natural pleasures of eating and mating—had been suspended, replaced by this abrupt denial of flight. Then there had been the struggle that shook the web, and the rapid approach of the terror that these silken vibrations had so swiftly summoned; finally the paralysing bite that had frozen life to a halt, leaving only the darkness.

And in the absence of everything they had known—as individuals deprived of life while yet they had no concept of death—these cocooned insects could only ask, "Why?"

Which was the "why?" that the Necroscope heard.

Deprived individuals, yes. But—

—In sharp contrast, three inches underground, in a sandy border at the rim of a path where the crazy-paving was cracked, the bodies of a veritable community, an almost entire colony of one of Nature's smallest ant species—insects only a few millimetres in length—were heaped in what was meant to have been a last-ditch attempt at providing a protective phalanx around a pile of glistening, tiny white eggs. The colony had been killed off by Jimmy Collins after he noticed a lot of ant activity and all the damage their excavations were doing to his path. It was truly astonishing that anything so insignificant could make any impression on the world at all, but small heaps of soil and the dust of crumbling mortar were ample evidence of just how effective the ants had been in undermining his garden path.

Also evident (at least to the Necroscope) the massed cry of distress and total panic that Harry could "hear" or sense issuing from the poisoned hive. Faint as the deadspeak cries of the enshrouded flies, yet totally different in nature, these myriad voices had one theme, one concern, and issued forth as from the mind of one creature. "Survive!" that massed voice cried, despite that Jimmy and his insecticide had seen to it that survival was no longer an option.

"Survive! . . . Save the eggs! . . . Protect the young queens!" But of course, for they were the entire future of a hundred hives yet to be!

Not even a whisper in the Necroscope's mind—nothing more than intuition—yet still he knew that once again dead things were crying out against the immobility, negativity, and unknown darkness of death. But as with the cocooned flies it was knowledge he could ignore, *must* ignore because there was nothing he could do about it. The world seemed to be full of dead things; even the soil underfoot was made of dead things! And if indeed the Necroscope tried to accept or empathise with every thought, message, or feeling—with every ache or echo from beyond—it would surely mean the end of him.

And so Harry was having to learn to put this side effect—this parallel or ancillary phenomenon of his talent—aside and make white noise of it, as he did with so much of what he heard with his ears, just like every other human being whose hearing is not impaired. And he was succeeding, except—

—"Hey, are you all right?" Jimmy Collins' concerned query from the shade of the doorway finally got through to the Necroscope. Jimmy had been absent for a few minutes only, topping up their drinks in his kitchen, and Harry had half-dozed off again—or so Jimmy supposed. He could scarcely be blamed for believing this was so, for on returning to the garden he'd discovered his guest with his arms folded on his chest, head down, and hat low over his eyes, as still as a man deeply asleep. But in fact Harry had been wrapt in concentration . . . listening . . . listening . . . *listening*! If not with his ears.

Listening to the incorporeal, yes, but not to anything as inconsequential (however remarkable) as ant and fly murmurings; not now that a yet more remarkable phenomenon had arrested his attention, and not now that he recognised it as something very different and *very* strange.

"Eh?" Starting—giving a pretty good impression of someone freshly shocked awake—Harry jerked upright in his deck chair. "I . : . I must have drifted off again! So now you can see how it is with me. Like I told you, I'm still sort of shell-shocked. I can't seem to stay awake for more than a couple of minutes at a time." He offered a shrug. "But perhaps it's just that I'm warm and comfortable here, and the place is so peaceful and all. . . ."

Jimmy was concerned, and the Necroscope felt bad about it: that he had conned his old friend like that. But it was part of the action that he now intended to take. "I think I'll just—" he began to say. But Jimmy cut him off with:

"And I think you'll be better off taking a nap indoors! If you go to sleep with your mouth open out here, you're likely to come a cropper. It's just a fortnight ago that I got stung by a wasp inside my lip doing just that—falling asleep in the garden. It still hurts, even to talk about it!" But:

"No, I don't think so," said Harry, standing up and accepting the drink that Jimmy handed him. "I'll drink this, and then I think I'll go for a walk—towards Hazeldene, maybe? Get some fresh air into my lungs, see if I can shake off this dull sloth or lethargy or whatever it is." He took a long pull at his soft drink, almost finishing it in one go.

"Well, you'll know best." Jimmy shrugged. "You'll be going on your own, though. There are a few jobs around the house I've been meaning to get done."

"In which case I'll see you when I see you," said Harry as he handed his friend his almost empty glass, then stretched and grimaced before heading for the garden gate.

As Harry opened the gate, Jimmy's frown displayed his continuing concern. "Are you sure you're okay?"

"Absolutely," said the other. "You'll see. By tonight I'll be my old self again and full of the devil."

Finally Jimmy laughed, and said, "Full of the devil? Okay, but if you don't get too full, maybe later on tonight we'll top up with Old Nick down at the pub! That's if you're up to it."

"Well, maybe," said Harry. "We'll see." With which he went through the gate into a lane lined with a hedge, and headed for a stile that climbed over and down onto a narrow path. The path led off into knee-deep, grassy meadows with hilly ground rising beyond. That way, maybe two miles distant, lay Hazeldene's forested valley, which was where this other—but this other what? This metaphysical interference maybe, or mental static?—this other "sound" anyway, seemed to have its origin. But if only it wasn't so hard to pin down, so very faint!

Unnaturally faint, when considering its *human* origin! Even as faint, and indeed fainter, than massed dead-ant hysteria or deceased-fly musings. But what sort of communication could this possibly be? Which was exactly what the Necroscope intended to discover, and ASAP. More especially so because he knew instinctively that however remote or suppressed its source, this was a concerted cry of horror, which to him was the same as an SOS: a cry or cries for help.

But an SOS from the grave? Now what could the dead have to fear? A question which only the Necroscope could answer. And in fact he knew that there were indeed things that the dead should fear, for he had met up with several of them before. . . .

The sun blazed down, and even under the wide brim of his floppy hat Harry felt its heat. Using a handkerchief to mop sweat from the back of his neck, he sought respite on a bench in the shade of a flowering elder. Having crossed the fields to the high back road, he could now look down across Harden to the landmark viaduct and the North Sea that sprawled beyond. The sea, once grey from coalmine spoil, was bluer than Harry had seen it in a long time; but then he hadn't been back this way since . . . how long? Last summer, perhaps? The one before that? In any case, he knew the blue was simply the reflection of a mainly cloudless sky.

The western horizon, on the other hand, saw that same blue sky merging with a bank of green: the rim of the densely wooded valley of Hazeldene, which was the Necroscope's destination and the source of those infinitely faint whispers that continued to sound in his mind. For the moment he tried to ignore the apparent desperation, the subdued terror in those whispers. What use listening to the unknown dead ones in question when he couldn't talk to them? He had tried that already but they didn't seem to hear him. Harry sensed—he "knew," by virtue of his fantastic intuitive talent— that they were close, only a few miles away; and yet they sounded as distant as could be. It was the strangest thing and quite beyond every previous experience. . . .

The back road, hedged and narrow, had grass verges. Apart from a police car parked some fifty yards away half-on, half-off the road, where three-bar fencing broke the hedge's monotony, there were no other vehicles in sight. Harry assumed that the patrol-man was taking a break nearby, perhaps relieving himself behind the hedge. What else would a policeman be doing out here in the open countryside, where there was little or nothing to police?

Moving away from the Necroscope towards near-distant Black-hill Colliery, a young man and his girl ambled arm in arm. From the opposite direction, closing with the couple, a pair of teenage colliery youths—their flat caps jutting and their hands thrust deep in their trouser pockets—slouched along the grass verge. Harry, where he enjoyed for the moment the elder's shade and a soft salt breeze wafting in off the sea, gradually became aware of the coarse sniggering of these two youths as they drew level with the young couple; but suddenly he found himself listening far more intently, no longer to the faint and mysterious murmurings of the dead but to the lewd, uncouth comments of the living—in the shape of this pair of louts.

Just a moment ago the largest and ugliest of these village types had taken his cap off and addressed the young couple with the words: "Oh, *hello* there! Lovely day for a country walk, eh? Out for a sneaky shag in the long grass, are we? Eh? Eh?"

And his smaller, stockier companion had grinned and added: "Can we watch? I mean, maybe we could help you out a bit if you get, er, *stuck* or something?"

"Why you dirty—!" Outraged, the young man let go his companion's arm, placed himself in front of her, and faced the pair of troublemakers. It was immediately apparent, however, that he would be no match for them. He was tall but spindly, and by his looks and actions—his rapidly reddening face and clumsy, uncertain movements—by no means a fighter. As for the thugs:

They had received the response they'd been looking for and their hands were out of their pockets now, clenched into fists. The biggest of the two had thrust himself forward, grabbed hold of and bunched up his potential victim's shirt.

"What's that you say?" he snarled. "Did you call us dirty, you soft-looking prat? I mean, did you call *me* dirty? See, this is just us having a bit of fun—*fuckhead!* We wouldn't want to fuck your stupid tart. Personally I'd rather fuck you—except you'd probably split in two! What do you say to that? Eh? Eh?"

By which time the Necroscope was on his feet and half-way across the distance between the bench and this ugly and totally unanticipated confrontation. As he went, however, he found time to speak to a friend of his in the cemetery near his old school in the village:

Sergeant, are you getting any of this?

All of it, Harry, through your eyes! Sergeant replied, and the Necroscope sensed a grim however incorporeal nod. *You could maybe use some help, but from the looks of these two bully boys only a very little help. And by the way: good day to you, too!*

Er, I was going to come and look you up, said Harry truthfully if belatedly. *In fact there are several old friends close by who I've yet to talk to.*

It's okay, no sweat, Sergeant answered, and the Necroscope sensed the grin he'd be wearing if he still had a face on which to wear it. *But hey, do you want me to handle this? If so you'd better let me in.*

Harry opened his mind to him—opened it all the way—and at once felt the other's presence like a mild electric shock in his body and all his limbs. By which time he had almost reached the four people where they faced each other off.

The smallest of the two thugs had become aware of his approach and said, "Hey, Jim, will you look what's here? Some kind

29

of twat in a hat!" With which he burst into sniggering laughter and did a funny little foot-stamping jig. "I mean, just *look* at this bloke—his flashing eyes and hard-man scowl! God, I could die laughing! Talk about the Caped Crusader to the rescue? Well in this bloke's case it's the floppy-hatted twat!"

"Eh?" said the slack-faced larger thug, releasing his grip on the young man's shirt and turning to look at Harry with dull narrow eyes. "What did you say, Kev?" Jim, who obviously wasn't nearly as clever as Kevin, focussed his eyes on Harry for a few seconds before bursting into guttural laughter like his smaller companion. And: "Oh yeah, I get it!" he said. "A twat in a twat hat, eh? Right?"

By now the Necroscope was within arm's length of the group. As he came to a halt and without preamble, he said, "You have a choice, you two: to either get on your way or to get hurt, it's up to you. So what's it going to be?"

"Eh?" said Jim—his favourite comment, apparently—as a disbelieving frown furrowed his forehead.

"Were you born thick, you fellows?" said Harry, grinning a deliberately caustic grin that he kept in reserve for occasions like this. "Or did it take a lot of practice? Maybe you studied for it in reform school, right?"

As it happened, however, they weren't quite that thick and the Necroscope knew from the way their jaws dropped that he had beaten these thugs at their own game, taunted them beyond endurance.

Jim and Kevin glanced at each other furtively, and yet in a fashion familiar to them; for they had known similar situations before. And as an unspoken message passed between them, then as one man they turned on Harry and lashed out at him with knobbly fists—which was an enormous mistake. For of course "Sergeant" Graham Lane was now a part of Harry, mind and body.

The Necroscope's dead friend, an ex-Army physical training instructor and a very hard man in his time—a man who had left the Army early to become a PTI for pre-teen schoolchildren, and who had died in an accident when Harry was just such a child—

had loaned his martial arts expertise to Harry on several occasions in the past and was pleased and eager to be able to do so again. Since the Necroscope was his only contact with the world of the living, however, this was hardly surprising; and just as Sergeant was into Harry's mind, so the Necroscope was into his:

Sergeant! he now cautioned the dead man. *Hurt them, by all means, but try not to break any bones. Please remember that I'm the one who might have to explain it if you do.* . . . Oops!

That last because Sergeant didn't appear to be listening.

Leaning back from the wildly flailing arms of the pair of bullies, Harry's supple body turned side-on and bent at ninety degrees at the waist away from his opponents. At the same time his right foot came off the ground, his heel stiffening into a club that his piston leg drove into the larger thug's genitals.

"Ow!" that one at once grunted, gentling his groin in both hands, dropping to his knees, and slowly toppling over sideways to the grass verge. And again, with feeling: "Ow!" as he curled into a ball there.

Sergeant! Harry warned. But too late because his body—as of its own volition, but in fact of Sergeant's—had spun like a top through a full three hundred and sixty degrees, his right leg extended and rising into a higher orbit. And once again his heel had come into crippling contact with soft flesh, this time in the form of Kevin's nose.

Blood and snot flew; as did the astonished, agonised thug, his arms windmilling as he landed on his backside in a drainage ditch between the verge and the hedge.

With both thugs immobilised and sobbing their misery, just as quickly as that it appeared to be over. But—

"Well now!" said a calm and mature, unfamiliar but plainly authoritative voice from behind the Necroscope, just as he felt himself beginning to relax. "And what have we here?"

Harry turned to face a uniformed constable in shirt-sleeve order. Despite that he appeared to be in his late thirties, the neatly-clipped sideboards coming down under his policeman's hat were prematurely grey; his eyes were also grey and perhaps more than a little cynical, as was his thin, tight-lipped mouth. Yet paradoxically, in a way that was hard-to-define, the aura given off by the man behind those eyes and that mouth seemed far less cynical than careworn and world-weary. Also—looking oddly out of place, as did the man himself—a pair of binoculars dangled from a leather strap worn around his neck.

"Er, I—" Harry began, only to be cut off by the girl he had rescued from an embarrassing, even threatening situation:

"This man helped us out when things were beginning to look bad," she explained. "And as for these two—" she indicated the pair who were still on the ground, "—they were acting like . . . like *animals*! They well deserved what they got!"

Her young man added: "I was . . . well, I was taken by surprise, else I might have been of some help. But—"

"But as it happened," the policeman cut him off, "I saw it all and this gent here—" he indicated Harry, "—didn't appear to need any help, now did he?" Taking out his notebook, he then spoke to Harry. "Might I ask who you are, sir?"

"My name is Keogh—Harry Keogh," the Necroscope replied. "I'm from Edinburgh, staying with a friend in Harden."

The policeman made as if to write in his book, changed his mind, and tucked it away again in the shirt pocket that held his whistle. "You don't have much of a Scottish accent," he said.

"I was brought up in these parts," said Harry. "I attended school in Harden." And after a moment's pause: "Look, I'm sorry if I'm in the wrong here, but I heard the filthy language these two louts were using and it seemed to me that this young couple were in trouble. Also, when I approached, I too was threatened! So it appears to me your time would be better employed speaking to these thugs rather than the ones they were insulting."

The other smiled a tight smile. "No need to speak to these two," he said. "I know them well enough. Work-shy hooligans, the pair of them; nothing they like better than causing trouble for decent, hardworking people." He scowled at the thugs where they were beginning to crawl away along the grass verge, then asked: "Do you want to bring charges, any of you?"

Feeling relieved, Harry shook his head. "I'm not sure it's necessary. I think they've learned a lesson."

And the young man asked, "What do you suggest, Constable?"

The policeman chewed his lip, thought it over, and finally said, "I think you should let it go. Twenty years ago it's possible I might have wheeled them down to the station and let them spend a night in the cells. They'd get out tomorrow each with a black eye, a fat lip, and a few bruises, and that would be that. Today, however, it doesn't work like that. The do-gooders would be yelling about police brutality and all that rubbish, and I'd be the one to end up in the dock. And—" he turned to stare at Harry, "—so would you, Mr. Keogh."

The louts had got to their feet and were limping painfully away. The constable called after them, "You two: I know you, Jim Carter, Kevin Quillern, and I saw what happened here. Any loose talk, accusation, complaints from you two, you'll answer for it in court, believe me. So consider yourselves fortunate, and now bugger off and quick about it!" Far less threateningly, he then turned to Harry and the young couple, saying, "Do please excuse the bad language, though it wasn't nearly as bad as theirs!"

"Can we get on our way now?" the young man asked.

"After you've told me your names," said the policeman. "In case it later turns out that I need them."

"Alex Munroe," the other replied. "I'm from Easingham. And this is my fiancée, Gloria Stafford, also from Easingham."

"Good enough," the policeman nodded. "You can go. I'm only sorry you've been troubled."

The girl turned to Harry. "You're very kind and brave, Mr. Keogh, to have stepped in like that. Thank you very much."

"Er, you're welcome," said the Necroscope. "But really, it wasn't much. I mean, I didn't have a lot to do."

Barely anything, in fact, said Sergeant, receding from his mind and body.

As the young couple moved off, the constable said, "Do you mind telling me where you learned to do that—your karate, or whatever it was?"

Harry had to think fast, but why tell lies? "My instructor was an ex-Army PTI," he said. "He died in an accident some time ago." And giving Sergeant his due: "He was a Black Belt in some disciplines and exceptional in many more. As for my own skills: well, for what it's worth, they're all down to my knowing him."

"He obviously taught you well," said the other. "I wish I was half as good! What were you doing up here?"

"Just walking," Harry answered, with a shrug. "Heading for Hazeldene. A bit of nostalgia, perhaps? I used to play there as a child."

As they set off back towards the parked car, the constable volunteered, "I'm Jack Forester—the lesser half of local law enforcement. The greater half is the senior officer I share the workload with. Actually, today is my day off—but I had nothing better to do."

And Harry thought, *What, no home life? Nothing outside of your work? Now that is dedication! Or is it something else?* But he nodded and out loud said, "I can remember the police station being close to my old school—Harden's Secondary Modern Boy's—down towards the viaduct."

"Yes, and the school is still there," said Forester. "But the police station is only a police post now. We still get some petty crime— sometimes not quite so petty—but when it's big stuff the detectives or reinforcements drive in from Hartlepool or Sunderland. It's all down to communications really. You see, Harry, in villages like Harden the computer age has put many of us out of business, and I suppose I'm fortunate to still have a job! . . . I take it it's okay to call you Harry?"

"By all means," said the Necroscope. And more boldly: "May I ask why *you* were out here, er, Jack? I mean, with your binoculars and all?"

Glancing at him through narrowed eyes, Forester said, "Oh, I was just keeping my eyes on things, you know . . . ?" And quickly changing the subject: "Look, I'm taking the old farm track past Hazeldene right now, so if you'd like a ride . . . ?"

Harry shook his head. "Thanks, but no thanks. I think I'll enjoy the walk." Actually, and if he wanted to, he could get to his destination long before the policeman, but that wasn't something he was about to mention.

"Suit yourself," said Forester, getting into his car. "And let's hope you have no more trouble from local louts, eh? But I should warn you, these days we have more than our fair share of them. Plenty of crazy people, too!"

Harry watched him drive away, but at a bend some two hundred yards away the car stopped and Forester got out. The Necroscope wondered if perhaps the constable was intending to have a few more words with the thugs; seeing no sign of Jim and Kevin, however, something warned Harry to step into a gap in the hedge where he could watch Forester without himself being seen.

And when he peered out along the road:

There was the constable, standing tall on the top step of a stile, staring intently towards Hazeldene through his binoculars. At which Harry could only shake his head in wonder.

What, yet another mystery? It would certainly seem so. . . .

Most of the time, the Necroscope had no problem making use of a rather exotic means of transportation—in fact *tele*-portation—which he called the Möbius Continuum: something he'd acquired from another friend and mentor, the long-dead German astronomer and brilliant mathematician August Ferdinand Möbius of Leipzig. On certain fortunately rare occasions, however, when experiencing a mild form of paranoia, Harry would use the Continuum only sparingly; this was mainly out of fear of being observed during the operation of the thing. For it wouldn't do to be seen quite literally disappearing out of this world, or for that matter to be witnessed reemerging out of nowhere back into it!

Today, up until now, had been just such an occasion; Harry had so far avoided instantaneous mobility partly as a result of this paranoia, partly from a genuine sense of nostalgia. For he really had played in these fields and along these woodland ways as a child, and walking here again had conjured mainly friendly memories of his boyhood. The past, in which he had known little of the true horrors of the world—horrors he had now faced and must surely go on to face again—had felt far less threatening than the known present and unknown future. . . .

But now there were things the Necroscope must investigate, tasks which he knew could be performed much more efficiently by means of the Möbius Continuum. First he wanted to know what had so fascinated a policeman like Jack Forester that he spied upon it in secret, and he knew that the object of that fascination—whatever it proved to be—lay to the west in the direction of the valley of Hazeldene.

All well and good, for Harry felt sure that the source of the oh-so-faint voices—so *very* faint they might even seem to be calling from the stars—lay somewhere in that same sprawling expanse of gloomy, uncut woodland with its narrow paths and tracks known only to the gamekeepers . . . for the ancient forest was private now and belonged to a landowner.

And who could say? Despite the seemingly long odds against such mysteries being connected, maybe the Necroscope would somehow manage to kill two birds with one stone. *Except,* Harry told himself wryly, *where killing is concerned, I know the owners of those phantom voices are already dead. . . .*

As for how he would proceed:

Forester had been gazing not only towards Hazeldene but also in the direction of a cluster of derelict barns and buildings known to the Necroscope from teenage times as Bellingham's Farm. Now, in a short series of Möbius jumps, Harry would move as close as possible to the ruins and there, if only to satisfy his *own* curiosity, would try to locate the object of Constable Forester's. Successful or not,

Peabody Public Library
Monday February 6 2017 11:22AM
ppl.lib.in.us
Telephone (260) 244-5541

Barcode: 30403000201053
Title: The long lost
Due date: 2017-02-27 23:59:00

Barcode: 30403001257583
Title: The tattooed girl : a novel
Due date: 2017-02-27 23:59:00

Barcode: 30403001730456
Title: Necroscope Harry and the pira
Due date: 2017-02-27 23:59:00

Total items checked out: 3

he would then use the dilapidated farm as the first of three Möbius co-ordinates, employing triangulation to pinpoint the more or less precise location of . . . the location of—

—But of what? Best start thinking of it, Harry supposed, as the unquiet grave of a number—very possibly a large number—of terrified dead ones. Because for the time being he had no other name for it. . . .

The one known to the ancient Thing in the woods as the Searcher was close by. The Thing "sensed" the unmistakable essence of an enemy, a being bent on revenge: the Searcher!

There had been others scattered down the lonely centuries; as time passed they had all wearied of searching for the Thing, or they had simply grown old and died. Their lives were of very short duration, after all. This one, however, was very persistent. Spring or summer, fall or winter, he would be there, sometimes on the rim of the forest, at other times deep within, his scent radiating from him as it had on that warm summer day when he'd fallen asleep at the edge of the woods after embracing with a companion, and the Thing had stolen her away. Then, following a brief hiatus—a pause that was at least brief to the Thing—this one had returned as the Searcher, his essence changed from a warm, benevolent flux not unlike the bodily wafts and emanations of lesser creatures, to a bitterly cold flow of implacable hatred. His underlying scent, however—which was of the blood and so unchanged—had been instantly recognisable.

And so the cat and mouse game had commenced. . . .

The theft of the Searcher's companion that time was only the most recent example of the Thing's occasional requirement: the abstraction of sustenance of that nature. And it had taken place a good many summers ago; not very long at all to a Thing of numberless years for whom the very concept of time scarcely had meaning; in whose perceptions the seasons of Earth came and went like so many days and nights. But as for the Thing's periodic urge to satisfy certain needs in that fashion: it was only an "occasional" requirement, yes; for while it might feel tempted to indulge itself whenever the opportunity arose, a certain event remembered from the past warned of the potentially lethal cost of such feasting, if or when currently quiescent creatures should find a reason to rise up in anger and come searching in the depths of the woods for an ancient Thing.

And so, because even one Searcher was too many, the Thing knew to keep itself hidden away. The difficulties it would face if there were more of them—and the vengeance they might wreak if its hungers got out of control—simply did not bear contemplation. For the ancient Thing remembered the terrible heat and awful stench, and the crackle and whoosh! of the fire which had taken each and every other member of its species, offering them up to the stars in the form of so much smoke and drifting ash!

Which was not the way to go!

Ahhhhh! But it also remembered how very sweet it had been on those occasions when it had given in to its needs and urges, and it kept these memories fresh by prisoning its dead victims' souls so that it might listen to their undying cries of outrage and horror! Which to the Thing's way of thinking—in its cognizance or consideration—was by no means an act of monstrous cruelty. For emotionless except for those aforementioned "pleasures," it probably wouldn't even recognise the concept of malevolent intent. Does an octopus consider the ingestion of living molluscs cruel? No, it doesn't consider it at all except as the taking of sustenance. It is simply octopus evolution: a requirement necessary for the survival of species, the renewal of like kind.

And so, in the near future, when the Thing would reproduce and bring about the renewal of its like kind, then, Searcher or no Searcher—with all possible terrors set aside—its needs must be satisfied and another sentient creature taken.

But ahhhhh! It would be sweet again, and when all was done . . . yet another trophy voice adding to the chorus of those gone before, crying into the void that lies beyond life. And only an ancient Thing to hear and enjoy that chorus and the memories it brought—

—Or so the Thing thought. . . .

From the top step of the stile where Jack Forester had used his binoculars to gaze toward the ruins of Bellingham's Farm, Harry scanned the horizon in all directions and made sure that he was quite alone. Then, stepping down into the field on the far side of the fence, he moved behind the hedge.

It had been quite a while since the young couple he had saved from their awkward, even threatening situation had moved on, and Harry had allowed yet more time since the departure of Constable Forester's police car. Until at last, satisfied that he couldn't be spied upon, he shuttered his eyes, conjured Möbius math, and set the dead scientist's incredible metaphysical formulae scrolling and mutating down the screen of his mind.

A moment more and a Möbius door, invisible to anyone else, took shape before him. It was like a patch of utter darkness, a black hole framed by the real or physical universe; except this immaterial door—this portal on a "place" that lay parallel to all space and time which Harry had named the Möbius Continuum—was also very real, and he knew how to use the weird dimension that it guarded.

Harry had gazed across the fields at a near-distant hedgerow which he would use as a co-ordinate. Now he stepped through the door preparatory to going to the hedge, and saw that within the Continuum it was as it had always been: a nowhere and nothingness that yet held the secrets of everywhere and everything, the original and selfsame Totality that existed before ever God demanded, "Let there be light!" It was a "place," yes, which was the simplest and the only way to describe it; a place where the absence of physicality was utter, where thoughts had weight and time was nonexistent, so that not a single moment of the Necroscope's personal time passed between his entering the Continuum and his leaving it.

Now he stood beside a hedge which, the last time that he'd looked at it, had been a third of a mile away! While across the fields the derelict old farm buildings were of course that much closer. . . .

Still unseen, Harry conjured and used the Continuum again, and yet again, until he arrived at his destination. Except this last time, upon emerging as from nowhere, he saw how very fortunate he was that his coming had not been observed.

Constable Jack Forester's police car, parked with its door standing open, was the first thing to inform of the presence of others, followed by shouting and wild cries of pain or protest. Hurrying round a corner of fallen farmhouse wall, where a stone chimney stuck up from the debris like an obscene gesture, Harry stepped into the open. His sudden arrival, however, went unnoticed by the two who were there; they were concentrating on what they were doing: Jack Forester, sitting on and apparently beating a yelping, struggling, shabbily dressed younger man on the ground, and the latter fending off the policeman's blows while protecting his face and wincing eyes with his forearms.

"Hey!" Harry called out, moving forward. "What on earth is going on? Is that you, Jack Forester?" He knew full well it was the constable, of course, but felt he really ought to intervene in what seemed a very unequal fight where the young tramp—who or whatever he was—was sure to get the worst of it. Also, in Harry's judgement and from what he already knew of Forester, he was fairly sure that the policeman wasn't by any means a brutal man; which meant that some sort of explanation seemed in order. As he drew closer to the pair on the ground, however, it became clear that Forester wasn't so much punching the other as trying to slap him. Not only that but the constable was actually sobbing!

Coming to a halt in the dusty, rubble-strewn farmyard, the Necroscope said, "Oh!" because he didn't know what else to say. And Forester stopped his unproductive attack on the man beneath him, got slowly to his feet, and brushed himself down with shaking hands. Looking at Harry, he saw the Necroscope staring back at him; at his gaunt, dusty cheeks streaked with tears. And:

"The dust is . . . it got in my eyes," the constable lied by way of explanation, his voice close to breaking.

"So I see," said Harry, seeing nothing of the sort. "But I still don't know what's going on."

Forester stooped, picked up his hat, and positioned it carefully on his head before answering. Then, scowling at Harry, he snarled, "Just who the fuck do you think you're talking to, Mr. Keogh? I'm not one of your colliery thugs that you can practice your karate on. I'm the law around here and *nobody* questions me or talks to me like that!"

"No," said his younger victim, as he propped himself up on one elbow, "and nobody can talk *sense* to you either, that's for sure!"

"Why you filthy, twisted, lying—" Forester turned to him again, and for a moment Harry thought he was going to kick him. But then the policeman spun around and without another word set off towards his car. The Necroscope remained silent, watched him out of sight around the corner of the derelict building, waited until he heard the police car driving away. Then he went to the man on the ground, offered a hand, and helped him to his feet.

"What happened here?" he enquired. "What *is* going on? What does he have against you? And if it's that bad, then why didn't he arrest you?"

"Arrest me?" said the other bitterly, as he dusted himself off. "Oh, he'd like to I'm sure. But no, he can't do that. It's this double jeopardy thing, you know? And anyway, the way he is—the state his mind is in—it isn't his fault. I don't . . . I mean I *can't* blame him." And he shook his head.

Harry thought: *This man is quite obviously intelligent. He may look like a tramp: unshaven, attired in old, secondhand or charity-shop-soiled clothing, but that's just part of the overall jigsaw puzzle. Just another part that doesn't seem to fit.*

Now he studied the man more closely, albeit as unobtrusively as possible. Five ten or close to; lank, mousy hair; gangly limbs and a somewhat unbalanced or lopsided stance; and a long, oh-so-sad, deeply lined face—even an old face on his youngish body. So maybe he wasn't so young after all. Whichever, it appeared that he was aware of the Necroscope's scrutiny, and as if he'd read Harry's mind he said, "I don't fit the picture, do I? I don't look the type that policemen go around beating up on."

"No, you don't." Shaking his head, Harry again offered his hand. "I'm Harry Keogh. I lived in Harden and grew up here, but right now I'm just a visitor."

"Greg Miller." The other took his hand and shook it. "I *do* still live here, and some people resent it: Constable Forester, for instance. But, as I believe I already mentioned, he has his reasons.

Anyway, I'm thankful for your timely intervention. Not that he would have hurt me too much. He never does."

"Really?" said Harry, feeling utterly baffled. "Well look, er, Greg?" (But Greg Miller? A name that rang certain bells out of the past? It seemed possible.) "While I know it's none of my business, would you mind . . . I mean do you think you could perhaps explain some of that? You mentioned double jeopardy, which hints of a crime. Your crime, maybe?"

"You're dead right, Harry," the other told him, "it's none of your business. And as for explaining my 'crime': well yes, I *do* mind! So please excuse me, but if you don't already know the story I'm not about to enlighten you. It was a long time ago and . . . look, I've been called a lunatic far too often already! But just wait and see. Eventually it will happen again, and when it does they'll all . . . *huh!*" Pausing abruptly, Miller gave a massive start and glanced anxiously at the green wall of Hazeldene some hundred and fifty yards away. And as a puff of cotton-wool cloud passed unhurriedly over the face of the sun and the shadows grew longer in the ruined farmyard, so the colour seemed to drain from his face and he quite visibly shivered.

"Greg?" said the Necroscope, suddenly aware of an ominous darkening—not only of the light but of the atmosphere—and of an oppressive weirdness here. "Now what in the name of . . . ?"

But as the cloud passed and the farmyard was flooded with sunlight once more, so the other looked at him, shook his head, and in a husky dust-dry voice said, "That's right, Harry, don't ask—because you just wouldn't understand. You have to be able to *feel* it, to have *known* it, to understand it. Which is why no one else understands or believes in it. It's too . . . it's just too . . ."

He broke off, shook his head as if lost for words, turned away, and set off determinedly if unsteadily out of the farmyard in the direction of near-distant Hazeldene.

But while Miller couldn't know it he was in part mistaken in what he'd said, because Harry had definitely felt something. On the other hand he was also right in that Harry didn't understand

it . . . at least not yet. But for a fact Miller's name had found resonance in the Necroscope's memory, making a connection that
only served to increase his curiosity. And so:

"You think I wouldn't understand?" said Harry, following a few
paces behind the other. "So why not try me? I'm no stranger to
fantastic stories, Greg. I've heard—and done—some rather odd
things in my time, and I'm a pretty good listener." (All of which
was an absolute understatement if ever there was one.)

But as for Greg Miller: he wasn't listening at all. And as Harry
came to a halt so the other carried on, his gaze fixed on
Hazeldene's green border rising up unbroken beyond a field that
had lain fallow for too many years.

The Necroscope watched him until he merged with the rim of
the woods, then shook himself mentally and thought to return to
the other half of his original plan: to triangulate the phantom
voices. But alas when he concentrated, when he tried to tune in
on them with his esoteric talent, they were no longer there. It felt
almost as if . . . as if they had deliberately shut down. In fact he
might even take it one step further and say he believed that *they
had been* shut down, and that whatever it was that had controlled
or restricted their volume previously—causing them to be so
faint—that same power was now blanketing, smothering their
cries to total silence. . . .

Back in the farm ruins Harry hid himself away in the shell of a
roofless room, conjured a Möbius door, and used it to return to the
co-ordinates of Jimmy Collins' garden just inside the gate. The
high walled garden was exactly as he'd left it: with a pair of deck
chairs facing each other across five feet of neatly cropped grass.
Somewhere inside the house Jimmy was whistling as he worked,
breaking off now and then as he remembered the words to various
parts of a song by Elvis Presley, and singing them. Not a bad im-
personation at that, thought Harry, wondering what kind of songs
Elvis was doing now. Having been dead for a while, the King of

Rock 'n' Roll would have settled in with many of his own kind, musicians who had gone that way before him. But one thing seemed certain: whatever music they were playing and songs they were singing now, they wouldn't be dirges!

"Hey!" Harry called out—at which the whistling and singing at once stopped. "Jimmy, I'm back."

A few moments later Jimmy came out of the house. "Already? You couldn't have gone very far. What, a couple of hours, maybe less? So where'd you go?"

"Oh, towards the old farm." The Necroscope was deliberately vague. "But it was just too warm. Up on the back road, I got hot and sticky, decided to come on back. But something happened up there: I met up with this sort of scruffy-looking man called Greg Miller and . . . well, I can't be sure, but I seem to remember his name in connection with something or other—something bad, I think—when we were kids at school." For that bell out of Harry's past was ringing more clearly now, and he had indeed recalled something of an occurrence featuring a man called Greg Miller. Miller, a girl, and—if Harry's memory served him well—an incident that had outraged this entire north-east region.

Jimmy had been fixing and grouting some tiles in his bathroom; wiping his gritty hands on a rag, he came forward and sat down in one of the deck chairs. Taking the other chair, the Necroscope said, "So, do you remember anything about that?"

Jimmy screwed up his eyes, frowned, and nodded. "I remember something of it, yes. It was the talk of the town. I even heard my old folks whispering about it. Wasn't Miller a crazy man who murdered his girlfriend and buried her body somewhere in Hazeldene? And if that wasn't bad enough, she had to be the daughter of a local policeman!"

"Ahhh!" said Harry, feeling the short hairs lifting at the nape of his neck. "Yes, of course. And the policeman's name? It wouldn't have been Jack Forester, would it?"

"Forester?" Jimmy was still frowning. And now he shook his

head. "No, I don't think so. I seem to remember Symonds, Arnold Symonds. In fact I'm sure it was him, yes."

"You're sure?" (Now it was Harry's turn to frown.) "But we were just kids and it was quite some time ago; all of fourteen, maybe even fifteen years? So how is it you're so sure?"

Jimmy winked knowingly and tapped the side of his nose. It always felt good to get one up on Harry. "Because it was in the *Northern Echo* just a day or so ago," he said, grinning.

The Necroscope sighed and said, "Okay, Jimmy, go on. What, exactly, was in the newspaper?"

"A list of all the people who've jumped off Harden Viaduct since it was built in Victorian times," Jimmy answered. "It was a hot spot for suicides during the Depression. And I see you're wondering: why a newspaper article about that now? Because someone left a note saying he intended to jump, that's why."

"And did he?"

"No, the fool walked into the sea and drowned himself! But it was a suicide so they did an article on the viaduct anyway."

"And this Arnold Symonds," said Harry. "You say he was the father of a girl that Greg Miller is supposed to have killed?"

"A double tragedy." Jimmy nodded. "The loony Miller kills Symonds' daughter, and Symonds the local cop—who has already lost his wife to cancer a year earlier—can't take it anymore so throws himself down from the viaduct. The *Echo* carried these thumbnail sketches on all the suicides, including his."

"And Miller?"

"A loony, like I said," Jimmy answered. "A head case. They put him in a high-security madhouse, and a few years ago transferred him to the mental facility at Sedgefield. Until you told me you'd seen him, I thought he was still in there." He shrugged. "Maybe he's been cured or done his time or something. Me, I don't think we should ever have done away with hanging."

"No, Jimmy, you're wrong there!" Harry grimaced, shook his head. "It's a terrifying thing—the so-called 'dirty death'—to hang by the neck until you're dead. I mean, think of all the thoughts chasing each other through your head: the regrets, the bowel-emptying fear as the noose tightens around your neck, the sudden, undeniable knowledge that this is where everything ends . . . until it *really* does end, as it all shuts down and the only thing left is the cold and the crawling darkness. . . ."

Jimmy's brow had creased up while Harry talked and his jaw had fallen open. Looking at the Necroscope curiously—perhaps even enquiringly—he very quietly said, "Harry, I'm convinced! Heck, the way you make it sound, it's as if you've already *been* there! Like you're Death's closest relative, or best friend, or something!"

Or something, yes. Or even *all* of those things!

And glancing back at his friend, Harry thought: *I know a great many things about Death, Jimmy. Oh, a great many things!* He wished that he could say it out loud, explain it in detail; but anyway, who would believe him? No, not even Jimmy. Or possibly Jimmy, which could be worse still! And so, saying nothing, he kept the weird truth of the matter to himself—and also to the Great Majority—as always.

When it looked as if Jimmy might be about to question something else, however, the Necroscope quickly stood up, and said: "James, my most excellent friend, I seem to remember you saying something about a beer? So how about it? Are the pubs open yet, do you reckon?" Which seemed as good a way as any to change the suddenly morbid subject: a ploy that Jimmy was only too pleased to fall for, which left any uneasy notion conjured by the Necroscope's vivid portrayal of death to morph into a sort of mental miasma, a mist that drifted unexamined from his mind. . . .

Early the next morning, Harry rode a bus from Harden into Hartlepool where, in the *Northern Echo*'s dusty archives, he discovered almost everything he desired to know about the Greg Miller case. Much of what he learned corroborated Jimmy Collins' version of the story; but most important among several new items of interest, the Jack Forester connection finally came to light in an interview that the constable had given following the suicide of his friend and mentor Arnold Symonds. At last the Necroscope could understand and make sense of Forester's animosity towards Greg Miller.

The story went like this:

In the summer of 1966, all of fifteen years ago, the then-nineteen-year-old Greg Miller, a coke-oven worker at the colliery, had courted Janet Symonds, the seventeen-year-old daughter of Sergeant Arnold Symonds, who was the senior policeman at the police station in Harden. Janet had been a popular young woman; her charming personality had made her a firm favourite with the staff at the electrical goods factory where she worked in Hartlepool. Where Miller was concerned, however, Janet fell foul of her father, who believed that her choice of a man in "pit black"—a coke-oven worker—was a poor one; for of course Sergeant Symonds had planned better things for her.

Perhaps Symonds—whose wife of twenty years had succumbed to cancer a little over a year earlier, in the spring of 1965—was simply being overprotective of his daughter; or then again, considering the way things were about to work out, perhaps not. Whichever, Janet's eventual disappearance and presumed death by murder was the final tragedy that broke the policeman's will to live; more especially after young Greg Miller had told his side of the story, a tale which clearly amounted to a madman's "confession." And shortly after Miller had been locked away, Arnold Symonds took his own life by leaping from the viaduct's central span.

As to Miller's so-called confession:

That had been brought about by the discovery, at the rim of Hazeldene, of Janet Symonds' ripped and dishevelled clothing—in particular her underthings—which still had traces of Miller's semen on them. After that . . . it had to have been obvious to him that he must offer up some sort of alibi or explanation, or else suffer the consequences of such irrefutable, albeit circumstantial, evidence.

As for Miller's reason for remaining silent to this juncture: it was because he had felt that no one would believe him, which was more or less what he'd told the Necroscope only yesterday, all these years after the fact.

And as for the "confession" itself:

While admitting that he and Janet Symonds had been lovers, and that they had made love in the shaded fringes of the forest on the day she disappeared, Miller had insisted that he was innocent of her murder. But oh yes, *it had been murder . . .* or more properly the incredible semi-ritualistic entrapment and violent butchery of a young girl, of a sort seldom if ever witnessed or experienced by any man before him.

And the guilty party: that had been a monster, a nightmare in the shape of—

—Of the forest itself! A part of which had turned carnivore, stripped Janet of her clothes and then her flesh, tearing her limb from limb on the very spot where she and Greg had made love!

This was as far as the investigators had allowed Miller to continue with this sick, sexual fantasy of an account, which of course amounted to little more than a grotesque confession; and discovering the facts of these events now, the Necroscope could well imagine what sort of reception such a story—and for that matter what sort of treatment its author—would have received in these rough-and-ready north-eastern parts fifteen years ago.

And for a fact certain leaked reports of gratuitous police brutality, presumably the work of Miller's counsel, had quickly found their way into print in the local press—and had just as quickly been refuted. Not that they would have greatly improved the suspect's chances; having presented or attempted to present his "ridiculous alibi," the tide of public and judicial opinion had now very definitely turned against Greg Miller . . . .

Eventually, following the deterioration of Miller's mental condition into emotional chaos, various psychiatric reports had been prepared. According to one such, Miller was suffering from "a morbid degenerative psychosexual schizophrenia," a statement which the Necroscope believed must have played a part in saving the man from a life sentence. For with the exception of extreme and dangerous cases, society in general is opposed to the long-term incarceration of the mentally ill, by far preferring hospitalisation and psychiatric care; in which respect it appeared Jimmy Collins was correct to assume that Greg Miller "had been cured or done his time or something. . . ."

As for Constable Forester's press statement following Sgt. Symonds' suicide: there was more to that than at first met the eye. In its way a eulogy, still Jack Forester's bitterness was evident; he seemingly mourned the loss of Janet Symonds as much if not more than that of his friend and mentor, her father! And having met Forester—having witnessed at first hand his raging hatred of Miller—so now, reading between the lines, the Necroscope began to believe that he knew who Sgt. Symonds would have preferred as a life companion for his daughter Janet, and moreover that the man in question had in all probability desired to be just such a companion. It could only have been Jack Forester himself: Arnold Symonds' police protégé, and the author of this very statement.

More curious than ever, and determined to fathom the Miller/ Forester story in its entirety—and even more determined to solve the mystery of those trapped and terrified phantom voices from beyond life—Harry concluded his research at the offices of the *Northern Echo* and rode the midday bus back to Harden. . . .

During the half-hour ride, however, seated on the upper deck of the bus, with occasional glimpses of the North Sea on his right and mainly open countryside on his left, except where the route cut through once-proud colliery villages which now looked sadly neglected, the Necroscope found that his thoughts kept drifting back to something Greg Miller had said towards the end of their all too brief conversation at Bellingham's Farm. Miller's oddly cryptic comment, that "eventually 'it' (would) happen again," kept repeating like an echo in his mind. Or perhaps not like an echo, for instead of fading Miller's words seemed to be getting clearer and ever more insistent.

"Eventually it will happen again," the man had said, without specifying an "it" that had since become self-evident. "And when it does, they'll all . . . *huh!*" Which was where he'd paused abruptly when he—and in fact the Necroscope, too—had sensed that weird oppressiveness of spirit and its attendant darkening of the psychic atmosphere.

Following which, as if lured hypnotically or magnetically, Greg Miller had set off determinedly, however unsteadily, towards Hazeldene; towards that great brooding forest, yes, in the same direction as the currently undiscovered source of those massed, smothered voices from the darkness beyond life, or close enough to that source that it made little or no difference.

As for Miller's "it": assuming that the man wasn't still psychotic—if he ever had been—and that he hadn't in fact murdered Janet Symonds himself, it had to refer to whatever he thought had happened to her. His assertion, however, that this fatal attack by a maniacal forest elemental would recur seemed to Harry to indicate a possible familiarity with a recent history of such assaults. Which could mean that the man was indeed a killer and was hinting—perhaps even warning, however unwittingly or subconsciously—that he might soon be ready to kill again! Or, on the other hand . . .

. . . Was it possible, the Necroscope wondered, that what had happened to Janet Symonds *had* happened before but long ago, and that somehow Greg Miller knew about it? If so, how often had it happened, and how had Miller learned of it?

Perhaps there was a way that Harry could find out. . . .

Jimmy Collins had given Harry a spare key to the house. Letting himself in, the Necroscope found his host's note in the kitchen. A small factory in an older part of the village was urgently in need of a rewiring job; Jimmy's services had been called upon; he calculated he would probably have to work on it for the rest of the day, and maybe tomorrow, too. But not to worry: there was food in the pantry and Harry should just go ahead and use whatever he needed.

Giving it a moment's thought, the Necroscope decided that a ploughman's lunch—cheese and pickle, a wedge of crusty bread, and a pint of beer in a friendly pub; not necessarily a village pub, rather a town pub in Sunderland some twenty miles north of Harden—would do very nicely. Not that he had anything against Harden's pubs, but Sunderland had something that Harden didn't: an old museum, with a small reference library devoted specifically to these north-easterly regions. . . .

In his pre-teens Harry had visited the museum frequently; the contents of its echoing, dusty rooms had never failed to fascinate him. But in those formative years when his weird talents had been immature, undeveloped, the museum's relics—its many dead things, the fossils, stuffed birds and animals—had exerted little or no influence over him. Now, however, when the Necroscope could sense, hear, and occasionally even feel their incorporeal emanations, it was very different. But now too, he had learned to exclude such deadspeak babble from his metaphysical mind, much as he had with the plaintive insect murmurings in Jimmy Collins' garden. He knew instinctively which thoughts were from active—albeit dead— intelligences that had become aware of his warm presence and were attempting to communicate, as opposed to the abstract echoes and amorphous images of once-living creatures whose cognitive skills were even more limited in death than they'd been in life, and either responded or refrained from responding accordingly.

Not too far from the museum was a disused underpass whose shallow, arched-over recesses were a godsend for young couples on Friday and Saturday nights when the local dancehall turned out. In his middle to late teens Harry had frequented the spot himself, with Brenda, as they walked from the dance to the bus stop to catch the late-night bus to Harden, and he still remembered the co-ordinates. The tunnel-like subway wasn't the most hygienic trysting-place for lovers, not at all, but apart from the odd tramp, or some down-and-out sleeping off a drunk there, it would normally be deserted during daylight hours and so was ideally suited to Harry's purpose.

And indeed it was deserted on that early afternoon as the Necroscope left the Continuum and the shadows of the underpass, stepped out into sunlight, and made his way to a nearby public house. One ploughman's lunch later and he was all set to visit the museum, whose afternoon open hours were two till six. A few minutes before opening time he climbed marble steps to the massive oak doors of the place, where he saw a tall, thin, forward-leaning old man—who with his dust-dry, cadaverous looks could only be one of two things: either the curator or a local undertaker—using heavy brass keys to open the place up.

The last time Harry was here the place had been closed . . . but not to him with his esoteric skills. Remembering that visit now, and meeting the curator for the first time, he felt just a little guilty. This feeling, however, very quickly passed. . . .

Seeing that Harry was the museum's only customer, the only person waiting to be let in, the old gentleman sighed and said, "Well, at least *you* seem keen for knowledge, or you wouldn't be so eager . . . you wouldn't be here dead on time." Rambling on as much to himself as to Harry, finally he fumbled the great doors open and continued, "Ah, well—there you are—now we can go on in." And:

Isn't it just amazing (the Necroscope thought), *how often the word "dead" comes up in everyday conversation? Dead centre, dead cert, dead on time, and so forth? And right now, as far as I'm concerned, we really shouldn't forget dead-and-alive: as in "dead-and-alive hole!"* He meant the museum, which was beginning to look rather dilapidated. But then on an afterthought and far more cruelly: *Or perhaps it's not so much the place as its attendant—who seems far more dead-and-alive than his museum!*

But out loud, already regretting his silent sarcasm, Harry only said, "I came here quite regularly as a boy, but even then there didn't seem to be too many people using the place."

"Using it?" The curator repeated him, nodding thoughtfully as they went inside. "How interesting. Of course, the museum is here to be *used*, but in the main its contents are merely *viewed* . . . it is a curiosity as opposed to a resource. You see, microcomputers are doing away with small museums, just as television has done away with the radio."

So that was the old fellow's problem, was it? He felt that the museum was no longer needed—and possibly himself with it—and very likely correctly.

"I can see how you're probably right," said Harry. "But at least nothing has yet come along to replace books."

"Ah, books!" said the other. "But this isn't a library, my young friend. And even if it was, I think I would be correct in answering that even books are beginning to suffer; their sales, I mean. We do have certain very old manuscripts, of course, but all of them under glass I'm afraid. What exactly were you looking for?" Without waiting for Harry's answer, he headed for his office: a modern, aluminium-framed, glass-walled cube of a room looking completely out of place where it stood against the wall of this high-ceilinged, oak-floored anteroom.

Following close behind, the Necroscope answered the curator's question with two of his own. "But you do have a reference library of sorts? Even if it's mainly regional and dedicated to these north-eastern parts? I seem to remember doing research on Hadrian's Wall here; a homework project from my history teacher when I was maybe eleven or twelve years old. Actually . . . well, it wasn't so much homework as a punishment—and I hated it!"

Half-way through the doorway into his office, the old man paused and turned to face Harry. "Your memory serves you well," he said. "Indeed we do have a small reference library dedicated to County Durham and Northumberland; it's located on the second floor. That, too, is under lock and key, however, because of some of the rarer manuscripts. We've had more than our fair share of thieves, you see. So I'm sorry, but I shall have to lock you in while you do your research . . . er, though not on Hadrian's Wall again, surely?" Here he actually offered the ghost of a smile—but in the next moment was sober again—and almost apologetically continued, "Just give me a second or two to find the keys, and I'll be pleased to accompany you upstairs. . . ."

The old building lacked an elevator; as the pair climbed a wide mahogany staircase, then walked down an echoing parquet-floored corridor that ran the length of the building, they conversed. "Well then," said the curator, "may I ask what you're researching? Perhaps I'll be able to offer some assistance. The section you'll be entering isn't the tidiest in the museum, I'm afraid. I never seem to have enough time to put things straight—and I dare not trust my cleaner to go in there without damaging something. A manuscript is just a bundle of old papers to him—and given a chance I know he would smoke in there. Oh yes, I'm sure he would! And why not, since he smokes everywhere else? Even in the toilets, where the atmosphere is sufficiently, er, *fragrant* without that we need to introduce burning tobacco into it!"

"Well, you needn't worry about me," said Harry. "I've been known to smoke on occasion but haven't any with me. As for what I'm researching: there's a densely forested place some miles to the south. It's called Hazeldene. Some years ago a girl disappeared there, presumably murdered. I want to know if that was an isolated incident, or if—"

"—Or if, historically," the curator interrupted, "there have been similar, er, 'incidents'?" And unlocking the door of a room towards the end of the corridor, he glanced back over his shoulder at the Necroscope. "Well now! What an odd coincidence! And what's more, it appears I really can help you!"

"A coincidence?" Harry followed him inside the room, where he saw what the old man had meant when he said that this wasn't the tidiest place in the museum. In fact it seemed to be one of the most cluttered, with open books scattered across the top of a leather-topped table, numerous scrapbooks and albums of newsprint clippings lying four volumes deep on the seat of a chair, magazines and pamphlets of bygone times piled up totteringly on the floor, and shelves and pigeonholes where yellowing scrolls and other seemingly fragile documents looked in imminent danger of falling into dusty ruin.

Seeing Harry's look of dismay, the curator offered a sigh, shrugged, and said, "You see what I mean? Where would I find the time? It would take days—maybe a whole week—to put all of this back in order and get everything correctly located. Oh, the shelves are labelled clearly enough, but everything else is completely confused, a literary jigsaw puzzle where I might search for hours for just one piece! But as for *your* search . . . yes, I really do think I can help."

"A coincidence," the Necroscope said again. "You mentioned a coincidence? Can I take it that in fact someone else has been researching murders in Hazeldene? Was that your meaning? And if so, when? Years ago or more recently?" He already suspected the latter.

The curator dusted off a chair by the table and sat down, indicating that Harry should do the same. Harry removed a pile of books from another chair, positioned it facing the old man, seated himself, and said, "Well, then? Are you going to tell me about it?"

Tapping a long finger on the cover of a visitor's book or register lying on the table directly in front of him, the other nodded and said, "Yes, of course." And indicating the book: "At least I located this easily enough, eh?" And he opened the register to a leather bookmark.

"A visitor's book?" Leaning forward, the Necroscope tried to read and decipher the entries: signatures and dates, presumably a record of past visitors. But the curator was once again tap-tapping with a fingernail, partly obscuring the entries or perhaps indicating one in particular—the last one—a mere squiggle of ink at the bottom of the scrawled column. And:

"Ah yes! Here he is!" he said.

"And that's him?" said Harry, staring harder. "This other person, the one who was here before me? He signed himself in?"

"Indeed," the curator answered. "Oh, yes! Just as you must sign. But alas I was careless and never inquired as to his full name, and he only signed his initials: 'G.M.'"

Harry at once thought: *Greg Miller!* And wondered, *So then, if it really is my G.M. what did he discover here, if anything?* While out loud he asked: "What's the date? And do you think you could describe him?"

The date was some fifteen months ago—shortly after Greg Miller had been released from nearby Sedgefield Hospital's secure mental facility—and yes, the curator was able to describe the researcher, a description which fitted Miller to a tee. . . .

"The first time he was here," the old man said, "he spent two, perhaps three hours, then left in a hurry seeming very excited. The next week he was locked in up here all day on two consecutive days. I haven't seen him since then, but he left the place as you see it now. He kept a purple manuscript folder or portfolio containing some loose leaves, and a notebook with scribbled details of anything interesting that he came across during his research. I know this for a fact, because I looked in occasionally and saw him at work. When he'd finished here, I found that he'd taken his notebook with him but abandoned the folder. It's still here; I found it just a few weeks ago and I believe I put it somewhere safe in case he should come looking for it. If memory serves it still contains some of the material he was researching: mainly some old pamphlets by regional authors, a few loose leaves of scribbled notes, and some Second World War newspaper cuttings. But damn the man, why couldn't he just put everything back where he'd found it? For the Good Lord knows *I* haven't had the time!"

"You say this documents folder is still here?" The Necroscope glanced this way and that all about the cluttered archive, trying to spot something coloured purple. "But can't you remember where you put it? It could be very important—and not just to me. I think it likely that a great injustice has been worked upon someone, and I'll do what I can to put things right."

The curator stared at him for long moments, then said, "In which case I can only try to do my best, too. So then . . . where *did* I put the thing?" He got stiffly to his feet, joining Harry in gazing all about the room. But a moment later: "Ah!" he said, snapping his fingers, "But of course! Where else would I put it in order to separate it from the clutter?" And reaching beneath the table he opened a drawer. Sure enough, a heavy purple cardboard folder— more properly a reinforced documents case—was in the drawer, and the old man lifted it out into view.

The Necroscope could scarcely contain himself; he reached across the table . . . but the curator held up a hand. "First you have to sign my register," he said, "and then I'll leave you to it. And if what you're looking for is here, perhaps you'll take time later to explain all of this to me?"

"Well yes," Harry answered. "Perhaps I will." But when the old man passed the book across the table to him, the name Harry added to the list before dating the entry was "John Smith." It was a small but probably prudent deception.

"Good!" said the curator, without checking the entry. "Now I'll lock you in. The button under the light switch will summon me. When you're done, or before I lock up for the night, whichever is first, I shall let you out. So then . . . good luck!"

With which he left, closing the door behind him, and Harry heard a key turning in the lock. . . .

First the Necroscope examined a half-dozen sheets of notepaper bearing Greg Miller's untidy but mainly legible scrawl, and it was at once apparent that the man hadn't confined his research to just one library. Indeed, only half-way down the first page of spidery script, the note that first attracted Harry's attention referred to a visit Miller had paid to the British Museum's rare books department to seek out a translation of Lollius Urbicus' *Frontier Garrison*, an obscure manuscript circa A.D. 138.

This was not the first time Harry had come across Urbicus' name; he recognized it from that time when his disgruntled history teacher had punished some minor misdemeanour by requiring him to write an essay on Hadrian's Wall. On that occasion Harry had borrowed certain of his essay's contents from an Historical Society pamphlet published in 1911, entitled *North-East England Under the Romans:* A.D. *100–*A.D. *300,* by Alan Henbury. And Henbury had written of Urbicus as being an educated Roman nobleman who, having fallen foul of Rome's civilian government, had in effect been banished west where he became a governor in what was then the farthest of Rome's many far-flung provinces: in fact in the north-east of England. His *Frontier Garrison* was looked upon as being the fictional and indeed highly fanciful story of a roughneck centurion's adventures in and around one of the many forts strung out along the length of Hadrian's Wall.

And as Harry cleared off an area of the table in order to spread the remaining contents of the documents case more evenly across its surface, so he once again came across Henbury's very pamphlet. Brittle and yellow, still its thin pages seemed in no worse condition than when he'd last pored over them as a schoolboy; which, it suddenly struck him, must have been at about the same time as Janet Symonds' disappearance! And while the Necroscope was sure that this was nothing more than a classic example of synchronicity, he nevertheless found it oddly disturbing. . . .

Referring to Miller's notes again, Harry quickly saw how, until now, he had been following the man's trail in the reverse order. For it now appeared that Miller, too, had read Henbury's pamphlet here in the museum *before* journeying to London; indeed it must have been the pamphlet which inspired him to search out the Urbicus translation. And Harry now believed he knew why.

The answer, despite that Henbury had mentioned it briefly, and then only in passing, lay right here in his treatise.

Henbury, not unlike several turn-of-the-century contemporaries whose works had been known to him, had considered Lollius Urbicus little more than a fabulist; but it now seemed possible the Roman governor had been nothing of the sort! And the Necroscope was suddenly certain in his own mind why he—why Harry Keogh himself—had returned today to this drab old museum.

Not simply or merely to research occurrences in or around Hazeldene Forest, as Greg Miller had done—no, though that was certainly a large part of it—but also because lodged deep in his subconscious mind, having lain dormant there from that time in his pre-teen years, a vague memory had finally resurfaced in respect of something very important that he had stumbled across in Henbury's pamphlet . . . only to disregard it! But no longer.

For while those paragraphs that Harry had skipped over so blithely all those years ago had nothing to do with what he had been researching *at that time,* he now felt a genuine thrill of excitement in turning the fragile pages once again.

And there they were: Henbury's brief references to certain inexplicable, weird or occult occurrences—called "witcheries" by Lollius Urbicus in his novel—which the Roman governor and fantasist had used as plot elements with which to send his fictitious centurion hero, the "narrator" of various chapters, off on his adventures:

> Of these fantastic "witcheries" in Urbicus, there were several; most notably when: "A coven of Pictish sorcerers summoned from Avernus Yegg-ha, their gigantic familiar creature, who breached Hadrian's Wall and despatched with his bare hands, horns and fangs a half-centuria of Rome's finest, before the last handful of legionnaires were able to cast him down, put him to the sword, and separate and bury his gross, gory remains!"

But witches and wizards, or sorcerers, in Roman times? Of course, for the Romans were notoriously superstitious, as were most of the peoples of those ages. And an unfounded, unnecessary dread of these early metaphysicians had persisted not only down the decades but for at least a millennium and a half, and not least in Scotland.

Living quite close to Edinburgh, Harry had often visited the famous Castle on the Rock, where an iron drinking fountain and basin against the esplanade wall featured two heads—one ugly and the other beatific—and carried the inscription:

> . . . Near the site on which many witches were burned at the stake. The wicked head and the serene head signify that some used exceptional knowledge for evil purposes, while others were misunderstood and wished their kind nothing but good . . .

About this alleged battle, however—the "fabulous" Yegg-ha versus fifty trained Roman soldiers—Henbury believed that Urbicus had learned of the disappearance, and the presumed destruction, of a half-centuria of men who had been sent to defend an area of the Wall under attack by the Picts. Thereafter, Urbicus' fictionalised version of this ignominious event had been posited as an excuse for an unusual defeat, most probably the result of a Pictish ambush and slaughter carried out one misty night.

But this episode was not Lollius Urbicus' only "witchery," and among several others was the one which had remained as the vaguest of vague memories in the deeps of the Necroscope's unique mind. Little wonder it had taken so long to resurface; for as with Yegg-ha and others of Urbicus' "fictions," Henbury had mentioned it only in passing and it had had nothing to do with Harry's research:

> When Urbicus ran out of ideas for bloody battles around Hadrian's Wall, and other skirmishes beyond the Wall, on Pictish soil, he sent his "magnificent centurion, one Quintus Britannicus"—obviously a Briton, a hireling of Rome who, in Urbicus' fantasy, had risen through the ranks from legionnaire

to centurion—on various quests and escapades in northern and middle England.

As he developed the Britannicus character, that of a man torn between loyalty to Rome and the natural love of his own kind, Urbicus provided many opportunities for his hero to assist his often down-trodden fellow countrymen: such as the chapter where evil "forest devils" were regularly stealing away and eating the maidens of a hamlet some two dozen miles or more south of the Wall.

Having devised this typical heroic quest scenario, Urbicus then sent his somewhat heavy-handed protagonist to avenge these supernatural atrocities by burning down a huge swath of the forest in question!

We can be fairly certain that Urbicus' inspiration for this chapter of *Frontier Garrison* was inspired by an actual conflagration, details of which the diligent researcher may discover in contemporary records. According to such accounts as are available, this real forest fire occurred during a very hot summer and consumed many thousand acres of what was then a far greater, denser expanse than many forests which exist today . . .

And there Harry had it.

But man- (or girl- eating) "forest devils," stealing away and eating the young maidens of a hamlet two dozen miles south of Hadrian's Wall, which would place its location in very close proximity with modern-day Harden and Hazeldene? Surely it could only be a myth or a local legend that Urbicus had exploited. It must certainly seem so to anyone other than Greg Miller . . . and now the Necroscope.

For if Miller had served his sentence, been declared sane and released, and yet *continued* to pursue some monstrous, murderous Thing in Hazeldene's forest, then surely he was as crazy as ever, self-deluded and totally obsessed! Either that or . . . or he had spent all those years in prison for a crime he never committed, whose author had dwelled—and might even now dwell—in the gloomy heart of Hazeldene.

And if ever there existed a man who knew beyond any shadow of doubt that indeed there were ancient, nightmarish beings on and under this earth, then surely that man was Harry Keogh, Necroscope. . . .

Next Harry looked at a thin sheaf of newspaper cuttings, mainly from 1939–45 (instantly recognisable as the period of World War II), and found his conviction substantiated in that all of them treated of the disappearances of girls in and around Harden and the surrounding countryside; no less than three of them, who had vanished without trace, stolen from the arms of their lovers in the Stygian blackouts of German air-raids on the region's coal mines and coastal railway. But . . . his conviction? Yes, because what Miller had been doing now seemed obvious to him: trying to find a way to prove—if only to himself, since no one else was ever likely to give credence to his fantastic story—his innocence; trying to show that Janet Symonds wasn't the only victim of whatever it was that lurked in Hazeldene, but one of several or even many who had suffered the same fate before her.

And in that respect, at least as far as the Necroscope was concerned, Miller had already succeeded. Moreover, Harry suspected that both Miller's forest monster and the *something* that he himself had sensed in the woods were somehow connected, different facets, perhaps, of one and the same . . . but the same what? The same *anomaly*? For without a better understanding of it, how else might Harry describe it? Thus he had arrived at a juncture where he completely—or *almost* completely—believed in Miller. Except . . .

. . . He was also aware that it could be a case of "what came first, the chicken or the egg?" Had Janet Symonds' disappearance initiated Miller's search for evidence of its cause, historical facts which he might use to clear his name? Or had he possessed previous knowledge of the earlier cases, knowledge that perhaps affected the balance of his mind, causing him to perpetuate the horror? Or there again, could it be that he'd succumbed to some strange emanation from the forest, such as the weird psychic—and peculiarly sirenlike—whispers that had so disturbed the Necroscope?

Harry looked at the faded, brittle cuttings once again and had to smile, however wryly. Greg Miller may not be a murderer, but he was certainly a petty thief! The newspaper cuttings were all overstamped with the archival crest of the *Sunderland Times* and the constraint: "Not to be removed from these premises!"

It seemed Miller had been quite thorough in his search for evidence, until now—having gone as far as he could in museums and such, and convinced of his own sanity—he had begun searching for the actual villain of the piece in the gloomy verges of Hazeldene; a task in which it was more than possible the Necroscope could assist him.

Having determined to do precisely that—and perhaps simultaneously solve that other facet of this mystery—Harry would now return to Harden; except he wasn't sure how best to explain his business here to the curator, as promised, and as always he would avoid telling lies wherever possible. There was of course a way around that problem, but as for what the old fellow would think when he came to let Harry out of the locked room, only to discover that he was *already* out and the door still locked . . . !

Well, since it seemed unlikely that the old man would ever meet up with "John Smith" again, the Necroscope could only hope that maybe he, too, enjoyed the occasional mystery. . . .

When Harry emerged cautiously from the Möbius Continuum behind a bush in Jimmy Collins' garden, it somehow felt as if the time should be moving on towards evening; as if he'd spent the entire day in that dusty old museum room instead of less than an hour. Shrugging the feeling off as the summer sunshine warmed him, he put the sensation down to a combination of his relatively brief exposure to the museum's intrinsic gloom and, despite its total absence of time, the Möbius Continuum's utter, even primal darkness.

Entering the house, he brewed a pot of tea, took a cup into the garden, sat in one of the two deck chairs, and used the other chair as a table to support his cup and saucer. Then, trying to relax—for he felt unaccustomedly nervous—and slowly sipping his tea, he gradually settled into an uneasy reverie as his metaphysical mind took over and allowed the background "static" of dead voices to wash in upon him.

These were not in the main human voices, though the echoes of a few frightened souls—people who were only recently dead and couldn't as yet understand what had happened to them—were there on the periphery of the Necroscope's awareness. No, these were the revenant reflections of *other* than people: such as the massacred ants in their crazy-paving mausoleum, or the cocooned flies under the terra-cotta wall tiles, or even the frog spawn in a nearby ditch, where a pitiless sun had steamed away its jelly and myriad unhatched tadpole siblings to a gradually stiffening paste. These things—

—And then, suddenly, *something else!*

This time, because he had experienced it before and knew where to concentrate his mind, Harry tuned in on it instantly, almost by accident and before he was ready to receive it: that eerie sighing, those massed pleading cries from a place beyond life! No longer the psychic susurrations, the "white noise" of exanimate semi-sentients—but most certainly the pitiful telepathic petitions of human revenants trapped in a nightmare and unable to awaken or escape—the voices were, as before, even fainter than those of phantom insects; but they *were* the deadspeak cries of people! And whatever it was that the Necroscope had happened upon, he was now more determined than ever to put an end to it.

Yesterday (oh really? But it felt more like a week!) Harry had thought he might track down the source of the emanations by use of a system of triangulation: by taking a number of psychic readings from various locations around the forest and pinpointing the spot where they crossed. He'd been distracted from this plan first when he came across Forester and Miller scuffling in the derelict farmyard, next when the phantom voices had either shut down of their own accord or had been . . . but what, cloaked against their will? If the latter, it seemed possible that whatever power or agency had suppressed them had done so because it sensed the Necroscope's presence. And now Harry remembered Greg Miller's reply when he asked him what was going on:

"Don't ask, because you just wouldn't understand," the man had said. "You have to be able to *feel* it, to have *known* it, to understand it."

Well, Harry had felt something—indeed, he was feeling it even now, as it dawned on him that "it" might be feeling him!—so that he at once erected his mental shields to secure himself from telepathic probing. But too late!

He felt a sudden shock, a convulsion in the psychic aether— as if something had suddenly started awake—and in that same moment the dead whispers were shut off as surely as if a switch had been thrown!

Harry jerked in his deck chair, spilled his tea in his lap, and shot to his feet. Standing there in the enclosed garden, he stared west in the direction of the forest, glaring at the high garden wall as if trying to burn a window through it, picturing in his mind's eye the near-distant, gloomy, brooding expanse of Hazeldene. And despite that the day was still and he could feel the sun warm on his shoulders, he also felt that a chill breeze had sought him out, found him, and blown upon his soul.

Moments later, as he calmed down and used the flats of his hands to squeegee warm liquid from the fronts of his trousers, the Necroscope tried however cautiously to locate the phantom voices again—to no avail. Apart from the "usual" background static or white noise, he could detect nothing whatsoever; indeed, it felt as if the psychic atmosphere itself was dead.

And despite that Harry, as wary as he was, remained eager to regain contact—and for all that he continued to focus his mind, to concentrate, as the shadows grew longer in the garden—that was how things would stay for the rest of a frustrating, mentally wearying afternoon.

But only a little while earlier on that same afternoon . . .

As so often before during this long, hot summer, the old Thing in the forest had sensed the presence of the lovers, this time less than a quarter mile away. And as always it had vented its most powerfully seductive pheromones in the hope that something of them would drift in the right direction.

Those pheromones were the lure, the sickly sweet but irresistible honeysuckle "scent" that excited the lovers and, after they made love, caused them to sleep; and slowly but surely the lure was working. Five or six weeks ago at the beginning of the hot weather, the lovers had used to sate themselves in a favourite, secret trysting-place almost a mile away: a shady spot beneath the spreading branches of a tree at the rim of the woods, by a field lying fallow with lush grasses. And when the ancient Thing had realized how frequently the pair pleasured each other in that place, then it had determined to undertake a long, slow trek in that direction, while at the same time using its exotic musk to lure them towards itself. For it was the ancient Thing's resolve, its intention, that in this way it would meet with the lovers at some juncture . . . a fatal "tryst" for at least one of the pair, whose juices should be all the nutrition necessary to facilitate the release of the Thing's spores, alive and vibrant as the quality of the salty-sweet sustenance itself.

But for now . . .

. . . The Thing had sensed the lovers there in the afternoon, felt their nearness and seen how they'd moved that much closer, how its aphrodisiac pheromones were luring them day by day more surely towards their doom. And the old Thing was pleased—or it would be except . . .

. . . The being known to the Thing as the Searcher was there, too. But of course he was: he always was! The bitter reek of an enemy's essence, the

Searcher's plasma, was unmistakable; likewise the mental bile—the mordant flux of tangible, implacable loathing—which he felt for the ancient Thing. And day by day, he too drew menacingly closer. But after all, what could he do? How might the Searcher ever hope to locate an ancient Thing who could disappear into the sprawling bramble thickets whenever he got too close? Oh, he was a strange one for a fact: a different one who seemed to sense the old Thing's presence as no other of his species ever had. But then, the old Thing had taken the one he loved. That must be it: revenge! But never so strong, not in all the Thing's millennia of existence and experience.

Which was the closest it would ever come to an understanding of the nature of human love. . . .

But while love remained a mystery, the old Thing did understand determination: the same concentrated effort of will that so pervaded the Searcher, and which the ancient Thing itself expended to entice its victims. It understood it and even now, or especially now—in the still of the forest, where beams of sunlight filtered down to dapple the leaves with gold—could even feel it reaching to enfold, to explore . . . and to know?

But feel it? Determined curiosity?

The ancient Thing could feel it, yes—the intrusion of an outside influence!

An outsider, not the Searcher but some other—someone or some-thing else—something far stranger, far stronger. A rare force: a creature that listened, heard, was drawn to the voices of those gone before who now formed a part, albeit an unwilling and metaphysical part, of the ancient Thing. A unique mind that fastened like a leech to those whispering voices and heard them not as the grotesque "singing" or "chorus" which so entertained the old Thing, but as cries of protest, outrage, and horror from a place beyond life, from within the Thing's very mind. Unique, yes, this being—

—This intelligence that spoke to the dead!

As that alarming truth dawned so the ancient Thing lowered mental barriers over the voices that betrayed it to the strange new Power, stifling them however temporarily. And then, closing its mind to the outside world—concealing as best possible its psychic aura—it ceased its laborious locomotion and became as still as its sudden trembling would allow. . . .

At about 7:00 P.M., with the shadow of the house falling square on the garden, Jimmy Collins returned home from a day's work to find Harry still out there.

Sunken-eyed from his hour-long sessions of mental concentration separated by only brief periods of rest, the Necroscope seemed worn out. And because he'd spent most of the time facing west, his face was rough and reddened from an unaccustomed overdose of ultraviolet radiation. So that Jimmy's first words when he saw how exhausted Harry looked, were: "Hey, Harry—are you okay? I mean, you look completely knackered!"

Waving his friend's concern aside, the Necroscope replied, "I . . . I'm okay, yes. I went and fell asleep again, that's all. After you warned me about that, too!" Then, standing and allowing his shoulders to slump a little, he headed wearily indoors.

Jimmy was hot on his heels, and as Harry collapsed into a kitchen chair he said, "Look, let me fix you a coffee before I go and freshen up. I'm dry as a stick after working in a dusty attic all day. I was hoping maybe we could get down to the pub again. I mean, couldn't you just kill a pint?"

At which the Necroscope realised how dry he was, and also how careless, to have let himself become so totally dehydrated! "Well?" Jimmy pressed him. "What do you say? The first round is on me."

"I think we should both freshen up," said Harry. "So let's skip the coffee and get on with it—and the second round is on me!"

The pub was one of Harden's oldest buildings; with its bull's-eye pane windows, an open hearth, low ceilings, and smoke-blackened, exposed oak beams, it was very atmospheric. The haunt of old-timers, retired miners whose bowlegged gait and coal-dust-ingrained faces spoke however ineloquently of their many years of hard work in the pits, the pub's wooden chairs, green baize card tables, and tobacco-scented air seemed especially welcoming to the

Necroscope and his friend after the disparate trials of a mutually taxing day.

As they crossed the floor to the bar, Harry found himself drawn to peer into a shadowy corner beyond a small table where a wooden bench backed up against the wall. For a single moment a face returned his gaze, then quickly drew back out of sight; but not before the Necroscope recognized Constable Jack Forester. And he thought to himself: *How fortunate! Because there's something I'd like to ask you, Jack.* So while Jimmy ordered the drinks he crossed to Forester's corner.

"Hello again and good evening," he said, as he approached. And before the other could reply: "I'm glad I spotted you there in the corner. It will save me a trip down to the police post."

"Oh?" said Forester, his voice a little slurred. "And why, may I ask, would you be calling in down at the shop, Mr. Keogh? Or ish it—er, *is* it—perhaps, that you want to report something?"

Harry started to nod, changed his mind and shook his head, and finally said: "Well, yes and no—or maybe both: something to ask, and also something to tell." He drew up a chair and sat down.

"Something to ask?" said Forester, cocking his head on one side. "An enquiry? In respect of? But before you tell me, don't you think you might have asked if you could join me before sitting down? After all, it could be that I'm waiting for someone. And since I'm not in uniform surely I desherve—I *deserve*—my privashy, a little time to myshelf?"

"I didn't mean to disturb you," Harry replied, "but I find myself involved in something strange, and I think—"

"—And *I* think," the other cut him off, breathing alcohol fumes at him, "that what you're talking about, what you want to know about, and what you want to tell me, has to do with me and Greg Miller, right? I mean, it's fairly obvious that you talked to him the other day, and it's likely he told you a lot of lies and a bloody crazy story. Frankly, I think you've got a lot of nerve, Mr. Harry Keogh, coming in here annoying me on one of my rare evenings off!"

Attempting to stand up, Forester half-made it to his feet, staggered and sat down again. His forearms, in thumping down on the small table, caused a cluster of empty glasses—a one-pint glass and three shots—to jump and clatter, while a full pint glass slopped a little beer. Avoiding the splash, Harry jerked his chair back from the table. There had been enough accidents with liquid for one day.

"Damn!" said Forester, looking stupid, just as Jimmy Collins arrived with a pint beer glass in each hand.

"Er . . ." Jimmy mumbled, glancing from Harry to Forester and back again. "I mean . . . am I interrupting something?"

"Just give us a minute or two," said Harry, accepting his beer. "The constable is advising me about something. When he's done I'll be right with you."

Looking mystified, Jimmy shrugged and moved away, back to the bar. And Forester said, "I'm what? Advising you about something? *Huh!* I don't recall shaying I'd—"

"—Just an excuse," said Harry, cutting him off. "But if I can be frank too, it seems to me you're still punishing yourself over something: probably over the Symonds girl? How first you lost her to Greg Miller, and then how both of you . . . well, lost her?" He drank a mouthful of beer before continuing: "Oh, and by the way, I don't think you're a hundred percent sure he killed her. No, not by any means."

Propping himself in the corner and seeming to shrink down a little, Forester was silent for long seconds, then said, "If I was shober, I believe I'd give you another chance to dishplay your martial arts skills. And if I could get just one good shot at your nose, maybe it'd teach you to be jusht a bit more careful where you're sticking it in future!"

"Listen," said the Necroscope, undeterred. "I've seen some of Greg Miller's evidence that suggests he may not be as mad or as bad as you think he is—or was. For instance: did you know that during World War II, there were—"

"—Several cases of people, including young girls, going miss-

ing in and around Harden and Hazeldene?" Forester was starting
to sober up. Sitting up straighter he slid his almost full glass to one
side and began using beer mats to soak up some of the spillage.
"You see, Harry," he continued, "this is all old stuff that Miller's
lawyer dug up fifteen years ago." He shook his head tiredly. "It
didn't convince anybody then and it won't now."

"Oh really?" said Harry. "Well, it helped to convince me!"

"Then you're a fool!" said the other. "And anyway, who the
hell are you, digging around in all this . . . this rubbish? Some
kind of sensationalist reporter? A columnist for *UFO Monthly* or
something?" Breathing deeply, and shaking his head to clear it,
the constable made as if to stand again. Taking a chance, Harry
reached across the table and applied pressure to Forester's arm to
keep him off balance and hold him in place if only for a few more
moments. The man was an officer of the law, of course, but Harry
knew people in London with a great deal more power—not to
mention *Powers*—than any village policeman.

Perhaps at that moment—as he felt the Necroscope's hand on
his arm—suddenly, for the first time, Forester truly recognised
Harry's authority. At any rate he sat still, focussed his eyes more
surely on Harry's face, and said, "Okay, I'll ask you just one more
time: who or what the hell are you?"

"I'll tell you what I'm not," said Harry. "I'm not a reporter or
columnist for any sensationalist magazine. But I do have connections in very high places, and I am interested in investigating in-
justices as or when I come across them. And yes, I do believe there
has been a great injustice here. But unlike you I know I'm not infal-
lible, and I admit that the story in its entirety eludes me. In fact
I still don't know the half of it, and I'll be only too willing to listen
to any logical argument, any genuine proof of Miller's guilt that
you might care to produce. So, if you're still keen to knock me
down, Jack, you can forget about giving me a bloody nose and
simply prove me wrong."

As Harry withdrew his hand, Forester relaxed and finally,

huskily said, "I've had this stuff bottled up in me for a long time. I really loved that girl, you know? She was truly wonderful, my first love, and if I had my way she'd have been my last and would still be here. Oh, sure, *I* loved Janet, but it didn't work that way for her. Yes we were sweethearts for a while—at least I thought we were—but for her it was just kids' stuff, not the real thing. I was more a friend than someone she wanted to stay with for life. So that when Miller came along . . . well, she thought *he* was the real thing, and the change came quickly.

"Harry, you could never understand what that was like for me. To be so deeply in love—me, a young policeman and friend of Janet's father, having to watch him suffer because after his wife died Janet was all he had left and he could feel her slipping away—and me, having to comfort him but no one to comfort me, while they were out walking, talking, holding hands and . . . and doing God-only-knows what else, Janet and that bloody, that crazy Greg Miller!"

Harry nodded. "So Miller took your girl away from you. I'm sorry to sound so cold but that's what it boils down to. And it hardly makes him a killer. As for him being psychotic: maybe he was—perhaps he still is—so why not tell me the whole story, from your point of view, and then let me make up my own mind?"

"The whole story?" The other repeated Harry, his forehead furrowed, frowning. "Step by step, d'you mean?" Half in denial, he shook his head.

"Any way you like," said Harry.

"But isn't your friend waiting for you?" Forester indicated Jimmy at the bar, where he sat enjoying his beer. "Young Collins the electrician, isn't it?"

Again Harry nodded. "He'll be okay. He won't bother us."

Forester slumped down again. "Very well—but we'll do it my way. I won't tell you the story the way Miller tells it, because I won't have any truck with sheer fantasy! So this is how we'll proceed. You show me your evidence—or what you *think* is evidence, that tends to prove his innocence—and I'll tell you my conclusions, how I've tried to rationalize these things over the years. And we'll see how easily you can be shot down!"

"Agreed," Harry answered. But after thinking it over for a moment, and when he tried to begin with: "First we should—"

"—Wait a moment!" Forester barked. "First *you* should know that . . . well, that I think this may be—I don't know, how do they say?—therapeutic? Or cathartic? I mean . . . I'm not sure what you've got that no one else I ever knew has, but since you sat down I've found myself toying with the notion that perhaps I can talk to you. Maybe I just need to get all this stuff off my chest, I can't say for sure. But don't get me wrong, there's no way you could ever convince me of Miller's innocence. It's more that I'm going along with this to clear my head, get rid of all the rubbish that's accumulated in there. Which has to be better than continuously thinking about Janet and her father, poor old Arnold—unable to get it off my mind, the way he jumped—and keep finding myself sitting in my car, parked up there on Ellison's Bank, looking down across the village . . . looking down at . . . at that . . . that *damned* old viaduct!" He paused and visibly shuddered.

Sensing, understanding, the constable's meaning—that he, too, had considered jumping—the Necroscope could feel Forester's fear. And staring hard at him, challenging him to meet his gaze, he said, "Oh, really? And you think Greg Miller is crazy? Jack, the way you're feeling, what you're suggesting, that has to be the real madness! I understand that you loved that girl, and I can *fully* understand how her disappearance might disturb the balance of her father's mind—but you're not her father! And you were a lot younger, stronger, then. Are you saying that this has been preying on your mind for all of fifteen years!?"

Yet again Forester sat up straighter. He took a long swig at his beer, a very deep breath, and looked about to get angry. But then, letting all the air out in a sigh, he said, "It isn't all the time. But sometimes—up in the fields near Hazeldene, when I'm keeping an eye on Miller—well, I'm not sure why, but sometimes up there I can get to feel very, you know, depressed and sick at heart? I mean, I can start feeling so low that I really don't know why I'm alive, or why I would want to be. . . ."

Pausing to blink and rub at his eyes, and shaking his head as if to wake himself up, Forester finally continued, "But this is getting us nowhere and I shouldn't have interrupted you. You were about to say . . . ?" He had deliberately changed the subject, and the Necroscope knew it. But he also knew that the constable was right and they were getting nowhere. For which reason:

"Okay," he said, "let's start again and revisit this World War II thing: these girls—and sometimes young couples—who disap-peared during air-raid blackouts. You said Miller's lawyer brought it up during the trial, and I know for a fact that Greg Miller him-self has been at work gathering together a dossier of similar cases. But you spoke of such things as being worthless, no use at all as evidence. Now why was that?"

Forester nodded, and sounding a lot more rational replied, "Very well, let's deal with that:

"You and me, Harry, we weren't even born during World War II, and not for a long time after. Maybe we should consider ourselves lucky at that, because at the time a lot of less fortunate young fel-lows were reaching eighteen years of age and being drafted to go and fight der Führer. If you lived in a colliery, however, and had mining experience, you had a choice: you could always work down the mine, because coal mining was indispensable to the country's war effort. Apart from which, and a handful of other protected trades, there was only—"

"—The armed forces," said Harry.

"That's right: the Army, the Navy, or the Air Force. It was your duty. But as in every war there were so-called 'conscientious objec-tors,' though often as not their main objection was to being cannon fodder! And who can blame them for that? But there were also those who—all excuses aside—simply cut and ran. Maybe it wasn't always cowardice; perhaps some of them had what they considered reasonable objections other than conscientious. Those who had young lovers, for instance: girlfriends, prospective wives . . . people they couldn't bear to be parted from, who they felt the need to protect during dangerous times.

"And what better opportunity for the occasional young fellow to abscond, 'presumed dead'—as often as not along with a special loved one—than during one of those German air-raids, eh? Oh, a terrible thing, to be blown to bits by a German bomb! And yes, people *did* get blown to bits and go missing in London! But here, in the north-east, the collieries? Why, you can count the casualties, meaning genuine, *proven* casualties, on one hand! Okay, Miller has his dossier of so-called 'disappearances,' but does he also have one for all the cases that the Redcaps had to deal with?"

"Redcaps?"

"The Military Police, Harry, who were stuck with the task of tracking down all the AWOLs and deserters. They worked hand in hand with local police authorities, and I've read plenty of their notes, reports, accounts in old ledgers. You want to know something? Up until seven or eight years ago—all those years later— men were *still* turning themselves in! Middle-aged fellows who 'disappeared, presumed dead' in 1942–'43, the middle of the war years. Sometimes they had wives, who 'disappeared' with them! As for how they got away with it for so long—well, who can say? They changed their names, kept moving from job to job, brought up families . . . you name it. But the point I'm making, the girls who ran off with these AWOLs or deserters under cover of German air-raids and/or in other circumstances: they weren't killed by Miller's bloody forest monster. They moved away, went underground, that's all; they escaped from unhappy, unfortunate situations. Miller's dossier and the 'evidence' that his lawyer produced: these things were just a bunch of red herrings thrown into the mix to confuse and deceive. . . ."

Listening to all this, remaining silent as he took it in, Harry found his faith in himself and his own beliefs beginning to falter; but he wasn't about to give in. Eager to regain control, perhaps too eager, and letting the words tumble from his mouth, he said, "Did you know that Miller has even traced similar cases back to Roman times?" But having blurted it out, he just as quickly realised how weak, even ridiculous, that statement must have sounded. And so:

"I mean . . ." He began again, more cautiously.

But Forester was slowly shaking his head, peering at the Necroscope curiously and with the suggestion of a wry, knowing smile tugging at the corners of his mouth. "Oh, and now who's crazy?" he said. "What's all this, Harry? Another of Miller's 'dossiers'? What, Roman times? Now we really are scraping the bottom of the barrel!"

Harry sighed and said, "Well, while I suppose you'll find it risable, I've seen documents dating back to the second century A.D. showing how a centurion put great swaths of Hazeldene to the torch, set it ablaze, to stop a 'forest demon' stealing away young women from a nearby hamlet—which would just have to be Harden, of course."

"You know," Forester replied, "it's true I'm just another son of a miner, born and bred right here in the north-east, but if there's one subject I was good at in school it would have to be history. And the Romans—for all their achievements in the arts, empire building, warfare, their structuring of social and governmental systems—still they were probably as superstitious a so-called civilised people as ever existed. They stocked their religious or supernatural pantheons and demonologies with stolen and borrowed gods and devils from almost every race they encountered, and having been ambushed by 'foreign demons'—the barbaric tribes of the period—in every thicket and copse they bulldozed their way through in France, Germany, Belgium, indeed the whole of Europe . . . well, it hardly surprises me they credited the existence of monsters in Britannic woodlands too! What you should remember, Harry: in those days forests were forests. Coast to coast and from John o' Groats to Land's End, there were dense, fearsome woodlands almost everywhere. What? Why, fifteen hundred or more years later we were still building our fighting 'ships of oak' from those very forests! *Huh!*"

The constable paused—at least until it looked like Harry was about to reply—then said: "And before you start searching your brain for more 'dossiers,' you should consider this:

"Forests have *always* attracted maniacs, murderers, and rapists. I defy you to find a single wooded tract of any considerable size in the entire British countryside that hasn't at some time or other been the scene of this sort of heinous crime. And as far as I'm concerned Greg Miller is *just* such a madman, with Hazeldene just such a forest. . . ."

Pausing again, Forester drank a little beer to moisten his throat, and continued: "I think that's me done. So then, have I shot you down or what?"

The Necroscope shook his head. "No," he very quietly said. "And I still haven't seen any actual proof that Greg Miller is a murderer. In fact it appears to me he was convicted solely on the basis of circumstantial evidence. Oh, strong circumstantial evidence, I'll grant you that—based mainly on what they found on the girl's underclothes—but on the other hand, well, Greg and Janet *were* lovers, after all . . ."

At which Forester's involuntary groan was clearly audible; and despite that he had earlier acknowledged at least that much of the Necroscope's obviously hurtful argument, still it seemed he might be about to reply—in anger or denial, whichever. But at that moment Jimmy Collins returned to the corner table, and his voice broke the momentarily charged lull:

"Harry, it's your round. But hey, if you're busy I'll get them in again and you can catch up later."

"No, it's okay, Jimmy," Harry replied, glancing up at him. "I'll be right with you." And as the other returned to the bar, so the Necroscope stood up, leaned on the table, and looked the constable straight in the eye.

"Well?" said Forester, his voice uneven and breaking. "Are we done? We'd better be, because I'm not prepared to accept any more low, dirty blows."

"No more low blows." Harry shook his head. "But one thing

you should know. However it plays out—and I will be around to see it play out—I know for a fact there's something weird and evil as hell in Hazeldene. Miller knows it, too; he's searching for it, as I think you're well aware. I'll help him to find it, if that's at all possible, because I think it will either condemn him as the madman you believe him to be, or finally set him free . . . by which I mean *really* free, not just from some prison cell. And Jack, who knows but it might even set you free, too."

Reaching for his glass and gradually slumping in his seat again, the constable remained silent, sullen, as Harry straightened up and made for the bar. Glancing back at him, seeing him withdraw into the corner's shadows, the Necroscope had to feel more than a little sorry for him. . . .

Mercifully, the evening was cooler than of late, with a velvety dusk falling as the pair got back to Jimmy's house, where Harry went directly into the garden while his friend made coffee. Out there in the garden, Harry felt the strangeness, the mysterious texture of the darkening summer air. It always felt this way to him of a summer evening, and even more so in the autumn. It was hard to explain: a feeling or emotion he'd always thought of as "an awareness of darkness as a presence," even as a friend. But he had never been more aware of darkness than right now, if for an entirely different reason: because what he intended to throw light upon, or into, wasn't at all friendly, welcoming, or anything in which the Necroscope might ever wish to cloak himself. No, for while the shadowy corners of this familiar garden might be harmless and empty, a certain greater darkness *out there* was something else, and it harboured something darker still.

Having twice sensed this thing in the near-distant forest, Harry knew where to "look"; the only difference this third time would be that he now knew it—whatever "it" was—could also sense him! Following his most recent effort, and aware now that the thing wasn't about to offer itself up for any lengthy examination, he reasoned that if he intended to fix its latitude in his meta-physical mind he would have to be quick about it. Find the thing, retreat from it, erect his mental shields: the Necroscope's plan was that simple. And tomorrow morning, in full daylight but from a different base, a spot to be chosen from farmlands to the north of the forest, he would employ the same plan to finally triangulate and so discover the thing's co-ordinates, the source of those deceased but yet desperate deadspeak whisperers.

It should have been no more difficult than that, but as he prepared himself for what was to have been a quite small effort of will, so Harry became aware of a faint but peculiar musk, an odour not unlike honeysuckle or certain night-blooming flowers, which he nevertheless found oddly . . . offensive? Or if not offensive, unsettling? It reminded him—but he didn't know why—of rain, damp earth, and mould, and conjured to his unique mind vague but very disturbing half memories from earlier times that he couldn't quite place, like those terrifying nightmares which go completely unremembered on waking. And such was the instantaneous effect of this depressing taint that suddenly Harry felt that what he was doing was of no consequence in comparison with the misery he was feeling. Why, was anything of consequence anymore? He very much doubted it. What an utter waste of time life really was, and—

"Harry?" Jimmy Collins touched his arm, then jerked back a pace as the Necroscope gave a massive start. And: *"Damn!"* Jimmy cried aloud, arching his body away from the coffee that slopped from one of the mugs he was carrying. And angrily, "Now what in the name of . . . ?" But in the next moment he was conciliatory. "I mean, did I startle you or something?"

"Yes," said Harry. And: "No, my fault—sorry! I must have been daydreaming. And anyway, this has been a hell of a day for small, damp accidents! Did you get some on you? Hey, I'm sorry, Jimmy!"

But he wasn't sorry that Jimmy had come from the house and disturbed him, interrupting whatever had been happening to him. And while as quickly as that he no longer remembered why he had felt so down, he remembered only too well something Jack

Forester had told him: how sometimes, when he was in the fields near Hazeldene keeping an eye on Greg Miller, he would start to feel so very low that he really didn't know why he was alive, or why he would want to be!

And with that memory, almost as a reflex action—or maybe an instinctive, even a retaliatory one—Harry opened his mind to scan afar and to the west. The evening was cool but far from cold, so that the icy chill he felt as his probe touched momentarily upon . . . upon something *other*, something monstrous, which had even seemed to be waiting for him, was a chill of the soul rather than a physical thing.

Repulsed, the Necroscope's automatic, defensive retreat was even more immediate than his previous planning had called for! Even so there was time enough between the moments of recognition and withdrawal for Harry to feel the utter *evil* of an alien presence in the psychic aether, time enough to sense the vile satisfaction that the presence was unable to conceal: as if the darkness itself had smiled and licked its lips—

—Perhaps in anticipation?

Jimmy had already gone back into the house and so failed to see Harry's involuntary shudder, the way he drew his elbows into his sides, hugging himself and trembling however briefly. In another moment the chill passed—likewise the sickly-sweet musk, fading away to nothing—and Harry was pleased to follow his friend inside. But closing the door behind him and shutting the darkness out, he wondered what had caused his weird adversary to generate such a huge burst of satisfaction, and to such a degree that he too had felt it.

Some weakness in himself, perhaps? If so, and despite that the Necroscope's resolve remained as unyielding as ever, it was scarcely reassuring. . . .

The next morning Harry was late rising. Some few minutes after eight thirty the sun was well up, the morning steadily growing warmer. Jimmy Collins had already left, gone to continue and/or finish his rewiring job; but he had left the kettle full of hot water which would take but a moment to bring to the boil. This was good, because the Necroscope was eager to proceed with his own kind of work and had precious little time to waste.

Over coffee and cereal for breakfast, he contacted his dear mother where her remains lay in mud and weeds on the bed of a river in Scotland near a property where once she'd lived. He might have contacted her sooner but had wanted to avoid explaining the nature of his current investigations. Though many years dead, Mary Keogh was invariably, though not unnaturally, concerned for her son's welfare in a frequently hostile world.

Now, however, asking his ma's help seemed the next logical step. And coming straight to the point Harry requested that she enquire among the teeming dead in north-eastern burial grounds, to see if she could find someone who knew of one Janet Symonds, late of Harden Colliery, presumed murdered and illegally interred in an unmarked grave some fifteen years ago. After beseeching him to take care, Mary said she would see what she could do and get back to him as soon as possible.

With their conversation at an end, Harry went out into the garden. And with his eyes narrowed, his mind shielded, he gazed west; shielded because he knew that somewhere beyond the garden wall lay horror in the shape of a thing that should not be. For last night in his sleep, the Necroscope's subconscious mind had recognised or remembered an occurrence which ordinarily, during waking hours under normal circumstances, should have been apparent as it happened—*if* it had occurred during waking hours—which he now desired to prove one way or the other: either as a dream or as reality.

It had to do with his mastery of the Möbius Continuum; the fact being that whenever Harry established co-ordinates for new locations, their points of reference then remained as permanent fixtures in his metaphysical mind along with myriad locations he had used previously. And, since all a Möbius co-ordinate was was a location at an established distance in a known direction, once "fixed" it became immutable except perhaps for the negligible effect of magnetic shift, the minute creep of the planet's tectonic plates, or gravitic anomalies caused by the inexorable but ages-long carouselling of stars on the galactic rim.

Last night, however, the rules had been—or had seemed to be—broken; and now, as the Necroscope thought back on it, not for the first time. Indeed, yestereve's confrontation with whatever it was in the forest had been Harry's third; and since the unknown woodlands evil seemed to have intimate connections with the final resting places of any number of exanimate persons who continued to protest however feebly against some kind of forced confinement . . . then how was it that the Necroscope had detected the source of that evil in three *separate* locations? Co-ordinates don't move.

Harry was reminded, however paradoxically, of the title of a chapter in a macabre novel he'd read as a schoolboy: "For the Dead Travel Fast," or something similar—which was paradoxical insofar as the dead he was concerned with appeared to be moving slowly! Nevertheless and despite that the changes in the angles of the Necroscope's lines of contact had been very small, still the deceased whisperers did seem to be travelling! Or, assuming that in their inanimate state they were *in themselves* incapable of motion, was it possible they were being . . . what, conveyed?

It was a question which served to remind Harry of another story he'd read in his teens: "The Travelling Grave." All very fascinating, not to mention disturbing, for it now appeared he had discovered a very slowly travelling grave of his own!

And a mass grave at that. . . .

Back inside the house, Harry obtained a number from the directory, called the village police post and at once recognised the voice that answered. "Constable Forester?" he said. "Jack? Good morning. It's Harry Keogh. . . ." And after a moment's silence:

"Oh?" Forester replied. "And what is it now? Are you still determined to waste my time, Mr. Keogh?"

"A couple of questions, that's all," said Harry. "And they only
require brief answers."

"Is that so?" said the other. "Well I'll be holding you to that.
And anyway you'll have to be quick because I'm due out on patrol.
You caught me on my way out the door."

"Okay," Harry replied. "Briefly then. What is it you hope to
catch Greg Miller doing up there, in Hazeldene? I mean, it's fairly
obvious to me that you spend a lot of time watching him. And—"

"—And you haven't figured it out yet?" Forester's voice was
sour. "I'm working on the principle that one day I'll catch him returning to the scene of the crime."

"Ah!" said Harry.

"Also," Forester continued, "I'd like to find out exactly what it
is that this crazy bastard is *hiding* up there in those fields around
the forest, and why!"

"What he's hiding?"

"He buys these cheap holdalls, sausage bags from the charity
shops. I don't know what he puts in them but I've sometimes seen
him with one up there on the edge of Hazeldene. Of a morning
he'll have a sausage bag with him . . . come the evening when he
goes back home to his run-down place just outside the village towards Hartlepool, the bag will have disappeared. It's happened
three or four times that I know of, but I've never been able to discover how he disposes of them. It's possible he buries them, but . . ."
The constable paused—

"—But that's enough. And now I have to go."

"Wait!" said the Necroscope. "One more question. You told me
you sometimes feel very low up in the fields near Hazeldene. But
have you ever noticed a strange smell? I mean, like a—I don't
know—like a sad sort of odour? More a feeling or sensation than a
true smell? Something that somehow reminds you of things you'd
rather forget? A sickly-sweet—"

"—Like honeysuckle and shit?" Forester cut him off. "Two

smells in one? Yes—and I don't much like it. It has to be the forest, tree pollen and the like. Blackberry blossoms and crabapple, too. And the shitty stink is animal dung . . . well, probably."

Even though Forester couldn't see him, Harry found himself shaking his head. "There are no blackberry blossoms—or crabapples, for that matter—not this early in the year," he said. "In another two or three weeks, then maybe. But not just yet."

Harry sensed the other's shrug—and that it was an uneasy shrug—more like an itch that the constable couldn't get at to scratch. "Then it must be like I've said," Forester said. "Just honeysuckle and shit."

"I suppose so." The Necroscope nodded, if only to himself. And echoing the constable: "Well, probably." At which:

"Careful Harry," said Forester. "Or you'll wake up one day as crazy as Greg Miller." With which he put the phone down. . . .

And now it was time.

Harry went back out into the garden and gazed west—seemingly at a solid brick wall but in fact through it, in order to "see" beyond it—then shuttered his eyes and used a deadspeak probe to scan afar. *For one brief moment he found himself focussing upon a babble of faint, frightened voices in a pitch-black room* . . . which in the next moment was gone, voices and parapsychologically conjured "room" alike, as the darkness in his mind withdrew and he opened his eyes to a bright summer morning. And Harry believed he knew what had happened.

Whatever the connection was between the forest thing and a number of dismayed dead people—whether it was their custodian or jailer, though the Necroscope was sure it was the latter—and whatever its physical shape might be and however strong its metaphysical abilities, it was certainly *aware* of him and since yesterday evening at the latest had made ready to shield itself and shroud its prisoners' voices at the slightest indication of his presence!

As for Harry's convictions with regard to its nature: the briefest of brief contacts on this occasion had been sufficient to reinforce any previous, half-formed suspicions into the sure knowledge that it was evil. For in the instant of its departure he had felt that a switch had been thrown and a light turned on that dispelled the darkness and temporarily cleansed the psychic atmosphere of something alien and rotten.

And if that unknown "something" wasn't evil, then the Necroscope simply didn't know what was. . . .

Once again Harry's intention had been to locate the source of the dead voices, and if they had been calling to him in person and not just crying out in some kind of psychic wilderness, he would have achieved his goal. In the Möbius Continuum he would have traced the voices to their co-ordinates as easily as finding a lost child crying in a room in a sprawling mansion. As it was, however, Harry now knew the direction—the latest direction—of the voices and their tormentor, but not the distance. Gauging that would have to be an effort of trial and error.

Leaving the garden by the back gate and making a series of line-of-sight Möbius jumps, he moved to the cover of a hedgerow some hundred yards south of the derelict Bellingham's Farm and there paused to consider his options. The comparative "silence" of the metaphysical atmosphere by no means indicated a lack of activity on the part of the living; there could be couples out walking, picnickers in the fields, perhaps a gamekeeper in the vicinity. And as usual Harry's need to keep his talents secure from public knowledge was uppermost.

So perhaps it was time he employed the Möbius Continuum in a new if somewhat alarming way that he had been considering for some time. For after all, what better way to observe the lie of the land than from a bird's-eye viewpoint? And if by some freak of chance a ground-based observer should happen to glance up at the sky, and if Harry didn't linger on high for too long—not that the latter was likely; the branch of physics that governed gravity wasn't about to ignore his physical presence—he might even be taken for a bird or a kite broken free of its string.

And without more ado he chose a spot in the sky—in fact one occupied by the tiny speck of a hovering skylark—and used the Möbius Continuum to go there.

For a moment the Necroscope stood still on the air, scanning the land below, his gaze sweeping north and south along the eastern edge of Hazeldene. And attracted by movement, the first thing he spied was Jack Forester's police vehicle bumping along a farmland track. That told him what else to look for, and the next thing he saw—a little less than two hundred yards ahead of the constable's car and much closer to the ominous green of the forest, in a field where the track petered out at the edge of a deep ditch—was a lone figure with the sling of a holdall over one shoulder!

Greg Miller? It could well be.

These things Harry saw and then he was falling, with the rush of his descent belling his trousers, tugging at his shirt, and filling his eyes with tears. At that moment, any other man would have been fearfully aware of Death's rapid approach; but the Necroscope wasn't like any other man. And concentrating on the mutating equations of exotic Möbius formulae, he used them to conjure a door directly beneath his hurtling figure and let himself fall through it. . . .

And in the next moment, steadying himself, he stepped from the Continuum into the co-ordinates of his previous location by the hedgerow. In all, it had been a flight of just two or three seconds' duration; but in that time Harry had seen everything he could have hoped for, at least for now, and his unique mind had recorded several new co-ordinates.

He could now afford to take a moment or two and let Miller enter the woods, then follow close behind him in a Möbius jump. He would be well ahead of Jack Forester, with his vehicle stuck at the ditch, and hot on the heels of Miller, still heading in the direction of his brief contact with his unknown quarry. In fact it now appeared likely that Miller was following the same trail, albeit by some means unknown to the Necroscope. Perhaps the man had developed some kind of rapport with the forest entity, evidence of which Harry had witnessed when first he became aware of this dark alien incursion. Or then again, Miller might simply be following—

—Following his nose?!

For there it was again: *that smell, that indefinable odour that was more a melancholy feeling or perception, that reminded the Necroscope of . . . but of what? Of every sad thing that ever happened to him? Every worried, anxious, sleepless night he had ever spent? It felt as if a dark cloud had passed over the sun, and the entire weight of the universe was pressing down on him. Except this time Harry knew it was no coincidence, knew that it was connected to Greg Miller—definitely to Jack Forester and something in Hazeldene Forest—and now to himself. And he knew if he let it take over, take control, that he couldn't say what it might make him do. Because his life seemed so utterly pointless with this great black cloud hanging over him.*

What, on a bright summer day?

For deep down inside Harry knew that it was a lie; he knew that life wasn't pointless, that he had purpose, especially now that he was so close to an answer to all of this. And he knew a place where he'd be safe and free of whatever was doing this to him, probably to Greg Miller, and most certainly to Jack Forester: a place called the Möbius Continuum, where whatever it was couldn't possibly follow him, but from where he could pursue it to whatever end was waiting. . . .

The Necroscope conjured a door, toppled himself through it, and immediately felt an effect, or rather *twin* effects: one of negative gravity in the weightlessness of the Möbius Continuum, the other a sense of relief in his instantaneous freedom from alien pheromones whose message had been one of suicide. Then, growing angry as he wondered whom that weird biological miasma had been fashioned to target: himself, Forester, or Miller—or maybe all three of them?—Harry sped to the co-ordinates where he'd seen the latter entering the forest.

And there was Miller, frozen in an attitude of listening—or perhaps of sensing?—just a few paces ahead of him. But as Harry had stepped from the Continuum into the gloom of the forest, so the other had heard the crackle of twigs breaking under his feet. Crouching down, Miller spun in a half circle, causing his heavy hold-all to fly up and throw him off balance.

As Miller lurched, so the Necroscope grabbed the hold-all, yanking on it to keep the surprised man out of kilter. Also, he stuck his foot out to trip the other up, then fell to the leaf-mould floor with him. And with a hand clamped on Miller's mouth to stop him from crying out, he whispered, "Quiet now! I'm here to help you. I believe what I know of your story, and I think I know what you're trying to do. But we have to keep it quiet. We don't know who or what is listening, and our mutual friend Jack Forester isn't far behind us."

Miller grabbed Harry's hand and dragged it from his face. He shook his head and said, "No, you don't know what I'm doing; you *can't* know! All you're doing is interfering, and I've never been as close as this before. So whoever you are—" He blinked rapidly, frowned, and looked puzzled. "—and however you've managed to follow me so quietly, don't get in my way now! In fact, why don't you just get the hell away from me?" But for all that his response was negative, still he'd kept his voice low, which at least told the Necroscope something of just how close Miller thought they must be.

"But close to what?" Harry wondered out loud, which simultaneously questioned both Miller's cryptic comment and his own thoughts. And as the other shook his head again—this time in obvious frustration—he quickly added, "Because *I* can sense it too! I sense it, smell it, and I even know what it wants of me: that I should kill myself! But what the hell *is* it?"

At which Miller's eyes widened; he'd read the truth in the Necroscope's words, his voice. He grabbed Harry's wrist, sat up, and reached for his hold-all. Its zipper had burst open when it hit the ground and its contents were exposed: a vicious-looking chain saw, and a plastic container full of a liquid whose unmistakable smell lingered on from a recent filling. It was petrol, fuel for the chain saw.

Glaring at Harry, Miller repeated his question. "What the hell is it? This thing? Well *why* the hell do you think I'd need a chain saw, eh? I mean, what does one *do* with a chain saw?"

Harry shrugged, and answered, "You can cut wood, even soft metal if the saw has the right kind of teeth."

"Metal, no," said Miller, licking dry lips. "Wood, yes . . . except I don't even know if it *is* wood! I mean, I can't see how it can be, and yet it looks like . . . like a fucking tree! Maybe not quite right but close enough to fool you until you're right on top of it . . . or maybe right *under* it! So who knows? Who can say? But Jesus—as crazy and impossible a thing as it is—*it eats human flesh!*"

"So you don't know what it is," said Harry, barely able to suppress a shudder as he got up, dusted himself down, and helped Miller to his feet. "But you do know *where* it is, right?"

Miller shook his head. "That's the trouble, you can never be sure. It . . . it *moves!* It moves slowly, but it moves. I told them where it had killed Janet—where we'd fallen asleep after making love—and where I'd woken up, seen what it was doing to her. Then . . . it had knocked me aside, out of its reach, unconscious, and I had lain there all day. They found Janet's clothing okay but not the thing. When I finally worked it out . . . by then it was too late. I was locked up and no one was ever going to believe me. But since getting out I've never stopped looking for it. Chain saws? I've buried half-a-dozen chain saws all round Hazeldene, so I'll be close to one if or when I find the thing. Wood? Sure, they'll cut wood. But when I find that bloody thing—which could well be today—you can *bet* I'll be cutting something other than wood!"

Harry heard a car's door being slammed. Turning and looking out into the open through smoky shadows pierced by shifting shafts of sunlight, he saw Jack Forester, hands on hips, standing beside his car on the far side of the drainage ditch. Maybe one hundred and fifty yards away, the constable peered left and right up and down the ditch. He was looking for the easiest way across, obviously.

Miller had meanwhile taken the opportunity to pick up his hold-all and venture into the trees along a route that ran parallel with the forest's border, where the open fields remained barely visible beyond the low branches and leafy canopy of the outermost trees. Hurrying after him, but trying to avoid stepping on dead, fallen twigs, Harry said, "Greg, you told me you don't know where the thing is. Yet now you seem pretty sure of your—"

"Yes, and *you* told me you could sense it, too," the other whispered, cutting him short. "Oh, really? Well, as for myself, I've never felt it so close before—and getting closer! And I really *do* know this thing. I know and *hate* it! As for the feelings it gives off, like long-distance hypnotism: I ignore them—well, mostly. By concentrating my hatred, I can simply drown them out! So now let's just hold still awhile and try to pick up its rotten scent, shall we?"

Miller paused and held a finger to his lips, and shortly, in a small, hushed, quivering voice, he said, *"There!* So then, if you really are sensing it, tell me what you make of that?"

"I've been getting that ever since I set out to find it—or you—or both of you," the Necroscope answered. "A feeling that life just isn't worth it. I might even have got something of it the first time we met, after your fight with Jack Forester. But I know what it is now; or rather, I know *something* is doing it to me—that it's not my nature but something else's nature—and that helps me to fight it. Forester, on the other hand, wrapped in his own misery, he doesn't know, can't understand. And slowly but surely it's working its poison on him. I think it's been working on him for a very long time."

"Yes," the other nodded. "I'm pretty sure it's doing it to him, too. Makes him hate himself so much he wants to die, which is why he takes it out on me."

"And of course Forester has other reasons—" said Harry, "or at least one other reason—for hating you. Which makes the thing's grip on his emotions that much more effective. He feels even more worthless because he can't dish out the sort of justice he can't even be sure you deserve! Little wonder the man's so frustrated, angry."

Now Miller was frowning. "You really do understand, don't you?" he said. "But, er, Harry? You haven't seen this thing. I mean, shit, you can talk about it, call it 'it,' feel or sense what it can do, but you haven't *seen* it! I've only seen it once myself, yet I dream about it every night. Because I saw what it did. Because in taking Janet's life it ruined mine. And who can say how many other lives it's taken down the years, the decades and centuries? Maybe even Janet's father? I'm been told he used to come out here looking for her, after they nailed me for what happened to her. Old Man Symonds. Poor old Arnold, yes . . ."

Harry nodded. "That makes sense," he said. "His suicide, I mean. But you should understand, Greg, that I'm . . . well, that I'm very sensitive to certain things. Things other people would find strange to say the least. And I know the beast you're hunting does a lot more to its prey than just kill and eat them. It may sound like a cliché, but its victims really do suffer fates worse than death . . . *and* longer lasting! And because in a weird sort of way that I can't even begin to explain all of this affects me personally, you'll simply have to believe me when I say I need to put a stop to this thing just as much as you do."

"Okay," said the other, "I believe you—mainly because I don't have time to argue—and anyway, I could probably use the help. But what *you* should understand is that no matter how much you think you may know about this . . . this *monster,* you haven't actually seen it. As for what it is: animal, vegetable, or something else, who can say? But one thing's for sure: it's big and it's fast! Slow-moving in its approach, maybe, but big and fast enough to kill us both if it attacks! The last time I saw it—actually it was the first *and* the last time—while I was lucky enough to survive, poor Janet wasn't. So if you still insist on being in on this . . . at least you know what we're up against."

"Thanks for the warning," Harry answered, even as he heard the sound of a dry twig breaking underfoot somewhere back along their trail. "But Greg, this isn't my first dangerous situation—nor even my tenth. So now can we get on with it, before Jack Forester catches up with us and further complicates matters?"

With a simple nod as finally he accepted the Necroscope's help, Miller glanced left and right, then leaned forward as if to sniff out the direction. But in the same moment, passing him by to press on through hanging foliage where shifting, slanting shafts of yellow sunlight pierced the dust-laden shadows, Harry had already taken the lead. Upon which:

"Why . . . yes!" Miller told him, taken by surprise where he followed on behind. "It looks like this could be the right way! But how on earth do you . . . ?"

"How do I know it's the right direction?" Harry whispered, anticipating the other's question. "Because where you can sense or feel it, I can *hear* it—that's how!" Which wasn't quite the truth, because it wasn't the forest creature he was hearing but the dead-speak cries of its victims. No longer reaching Harry as frantic whispers, their voices rang out louder and clearer than at any time previously, which meant that at last the Necroscope could actually hear and understand at least something of their pitiful mass protest:

No, no, not again! Please God, not again! Not another poor innocent whose soul shall join us in our misery, crying out endlessly into the empty void! Not another victim—or worse still victims—*to rot in the body of the beast!*

But what did it mean? Another innocent victim, and possibly more than one? More flesh for the monster, and more souls to join the trapped ones in their unending misery? What was it the tormented dead knew that the Necroscope and Greg Miller didn't? What was about to happen—and right here and now apparently— that had roused these prisoners of the Hazeldene thing to such sudden, frenzied activity?

The short hairs prickled at the back of Harry's neck, and despite the warm, musty breathlessness of the forest, he felt a bitter cold wind blowing through the corridors of his metaphysical mind. For he had suddenly realized that the unknown forest crea-ture was no longer shielding its victims' cries of warning, horror, and outrage. No, for now in addition to this previously suppressed eruption of deadspeak, the monster's *own* excitement was becoming increasingly apparent!

But it was more than mere excitement that the Necroscope was sensing in the psychically charged atmosphere. He couldn't know it, but it was an irresistible craving, a drooling hunger; it was *lust* as no entirely human being might ever know it: *lust* as the alien *Power* that energized the ancient Thing's drive for immortality, the per-petuation of species. And from the way that Greg Miller suddenly jerked and staggered, gasping his recognition of looming horror, Harry knew that he had felt it, too.

"There! Can you f-feel that?" Barely breathing the words, still Miller almost gagged on them. "And can you smell it? It's that *smell*, Harry—that smell, or sensation, whatever it is—that I woke up to just before the monster took Janet! I'd given her an engage-ment ring that very day; she accepted it and for a few short hours was mine . . . until that thing took her. And now it's happening again, Harry! Now it *will* happen again!"

And Harry knew that he was right. In its eager, evil anticipa-tion, the thing had thrown all caution aside; like a killer whale in its voraciousness, an orca charging from the ocean up onto the beach in order to take a seal, the creature was at the stage where it utterly ignored all possible dangers. Indeed the *urgency* it radi-ated in this prelude to its feasting was such as to make the worst human greed seem insignificant, and it was so close to happening now that the Necroscope would swear he could feel a great black heart beating in the psychic aether!

Some fifteen minutes earlier, Alex Munroe and Gloria Stafford— that same young couple that Harry and Forester had rescued from an embarrassing, even threatening situation involving a pair of local thugs—had finished making love in their secret place, a natural arbour enclosed by brambles close to the forest's rim.

Every weekend since early May, and almost every day during the last fortnight, the period of their annual summer holidays, they'd made love in the woods, moving from place to place until finally they had discovered this totally private spot. Only let them venture out into the summer air . . . it was as if they were drawn here! There was this incredible quality of atmosphere: an aphrodisiac musk, a sense of sexual potency, and such was their passion they invariably exhausted themselves and fell asleep in each other's arms. Which was exactly what they had done today.

Having dressed wearily after enjoying the mutual pleasures of their bodies, now they lay asleep, curled up on their spread jackets and secure in the knowledge that they were all alone in this secret place, invisible to the world outside the forest.

But to the world *within* the forest—where the presence of one more tree would easily escape the notice of inefficient human eyes, and where the many shades of green gave assistance by acting as camouflage—the lovers were anything but invisible. And as for believing they were alone:

In that they were very much mistaken. . . .

Once again, as so often before, the lovers had entered the forest; they were there in the secret place that they'd discovered and called their own without ever guessing the help they'd had. For without the ancient Thing's pheromones calling to them they might never have entered the shade of the trees and found their love nest, might never have lusted after each other, never have lain naked in each other's arms in the first place.

One alien aphrodisiac musk to fire their passion and lure them into the forest, and another narcotic, almost opiate scent to cause them to sleep when their bodies were spent. These were parts but not all of the ancient Thing's arsenal, which it used as instinctively as a butterfly attracting a mate, or more germanely, as a flytrap fermenting its gluey nectar. To that extent at least, in the secretion and use of such poisons, the Thing's activities were just as much instinct as breathing to a mammal; the difference being that it worked with purpose, with deliberation, and its every action in this respect was and would continue to be premeditated.

Another weapon was a powerful depressant which kept at bay gamekeepers, poachers, and artless wanderers alike. Only let the ancient Thing detect an unwanted presence, its sphincters would issue jets of a chemical as light as air which it would waft as best possible towards the encroaching presence. And such was the potency of this aerosol that men would feel dejected and dispirited, only recovering when they'd put themselves beyond its influence. Then, should they return, it would be to risk repeated doses of the sinister colloid, so lowering their self-esteem to the point of suicide and occasionally, fatally, beyond.

But now, today, the lovers were there in their place and the ancient Thing had almost completed its wearying, seemingly endless journey of a little less than a mile. An enormous trek but one which, as the last of its kind, it felt obliged to complete—which it must complete—if its species was to continue in perpetuity. For while its myriad spores were close to bursting they were not ripe, and they never would be without a special ingredient that the Thing sought: the life-blood of a human being or beings. To spawn now—ejecting its precious, once-in-a-lifetime spores high into the air, only to have them drift to earth without the liquids necessary to sustain them until their flaccid rootlets had matured sufficiently to suckle on the oils of earth—would be akin to murder. Worse, in the Thing's case it would be genocide! But taking the life or lives of human beings, in this case the lovers . . . that was simply survival.

Or perhaps not so simple. For as with all sentient life-forms, certain incentives and inducements were inherent in the reproductive process. In humans it was sex—the exquisite if fleeting joy of the orgasm—and similarly, where the ancient Thing was concerned, the payoff from today's business, in addition to the survival of species, was to be its own oh-so-rare pleasuring. Except this would be the ultimate pleasuring: gratification more ecstatic and fulfilling than anything the Thing had ever known before which, when the materials of its victims were absorbed, would trigger the release of its myriad bloated spores.

First the old Thing would revel in the joy of the lovers' agony as its hollow barbed spines supped on their juices. Then, in a state of alien, orgasmic euphoria, it would flense them of their skins, liquifing and devouring their flesh and even their bones. And finally sated, as the crimson pulp suffused its entire being, so the ancient Thing would clothe its limbs in the flaccid, wrinkled remains of its victims.

Then, with their skins on the outside and their immortal souls—their unquiet spirits—on the inside, they would be trapped forever, along with all the other incorporeal captives of the Thing! And while its spore progeny took shallow root in forest loam, in time becoming sentient and growing to maturity, so the monstrous Thing would while away whatever time remained, perhaps centuries, enjoying the "sweet songs" or more properly the outraged cries of its victims.

This was its plan, the dream it had nurtured, and now was the time.

Its inexorable creep through leaf-mould and turf—which it ploughed in front with its five principal "roots" or stabilisers, and carefully covered up behind—finally ceased. Its lower "branches" reached out across a wall of brambles to cast a dark shadow over the sleeping pair in their no longer secret place. It trembled in a fever of anticipation as chitin-barbed tendrils with needle-tipped siphons uncoiled from its core to sway out silently over the lovers in their bower. And:

Ahhhhh! For if the ancient Thing in the forest could sigh, then most certainly this would be the right time to do it.

Except, of a sudden, it sensed—

—Intruders!

Or perhaps only one intruder; the Thing couldn't be sure. Its inflamed senses were confused, jumbled, disarrayed. Ah yes! It was the Searcher; the cold flux of his implacable hatred was unmistakable. Here he was, finally caught up with an old enemy, a monster who was no longer willing to play their cat and mouse game. No, for the Searcher had come here at precisely the wrong time—and he was now destined to stay here for all time!

Three of them, then: three victims to fuel the old Thing's pleasure and enable its spawning. And all of them within range, and all vulnerable to the monster's raging passions and diverse weapons. But the ones in their bower—who were even now stirring to the sound of crashing foliage and shouting voices—they would offer the least resistance and so must die first.

But . . . shouting voices? More than one?

About to begin its attack on the lovers, the Thing paused. A moment ago it had thought to detect only one intruder. So why now was the air suddenly vibrant with the cries of at least two of them? Two voices calling aloud, alerting *the lovers to their danger! One was the Searcher's, certainly, but as for the other . . . could it be the group voice of myriad captive souls calling from beyond the psychic divide? Well, possibly; for now that the Thing focused its efforts on more important matters, its long-suffering prisoners were more nearly free to vent their horror.*

So perhaps it was them . . . and then again, perhaps not.

As a precaution, the ancient Thing sprayed aloft several pheromones in copious amounts, diffusing the clearing with its poisons. There! Now let the intruder or intruders proceed with whatever was their business—if they were still able!

And it seemed that at least one of them was; for now this second voice was actually attempting to answer the cries of the Thing's captive souls! So that finally the Thing recognised its enemy: to its knowledge a being unique to the human race—this man possessed of a talent not unlike its own, who would now use it to far greater effect—this Power who spoke to the dead!

But what difference did it make? The scene was set and the ancient Thing's needs must be satisfied. Whatever else happened now its thirst must be quenched, its spores quickened, enabled, and alien vitality passed down to seedling progeny. And without more ado—aware that something might yet go wrong as lust gave way to fear—the old Thing draped its barbed tendrils over the waking lovers and began tearing at their clothing. . . .

For all the many horrors Harry had known—the fantastic, monstrous events and incidents in which he, as the Necroscope, had found himself involved in his short span of years—even he had never come across or even imagined anything like this.

At first glance the thing would seem to be a tree; indeed, in its inert or stationary mode it was almost indistinguishable from a tree. But its "leaves," looking similar to an oak tree's leaves, were in fact highly sensitive palps or feelers: *sensors* of atmosphere, pressure and presences, of motion and proximity. Its "bole," with a horny sheath that looked much like bark, was the body that contained its alien organs. In addition to stabiliser roots that provided its mobility and took sustenance from the soil, it had a mouth high in its body that it closed during inclement weather but kept open to drink the warm summer rains, whose thornlike, chitin-plated throat—on rare occasions such as this—it would use to ingest entirely different fluids. . . .

Like a sea anemone, the thing might easily be mistaken for a plant; it could in fact *be* a hybrid of both plant and animal, though it was more likely the latter. Not so much an anemone as an anomaly, however, the mystery of how such a creature came to be here—how it had *been* here for untold years and even centuries—was one which must remain forever unsolved.

For whether it and its long-dead sibling spawn had drifted to Earth as spores from some primal comet's tail, or had simply evolved here over immemorial aeons, Greg Miller's plan—while unintentional in this respect at least—made no allowance for any future investigation; not if he had his way. Which was why he'd equipped himself with a chain saw and the fuel to power it . . . and something more than sufficient fuel at that.

But as for the Necroscope, Harry Keogh:

He was no longer shouting a warning at the young ones, who were awake now and trying to fight off the barbed tendrils that were tearing their clothes and starting on their exposed flesh, tendrils which would very soon flay them alive unless the thing was stopped. Oh, Harry wanted desperately to shout but couldn't because he was paralysed! Not with fear, though he was definitely afraid, but *physically* paralysed! For a cocktail of potent pheromones was in his nostrils, his lungs; not just the earthy scent of the thing but its concentrated colloidal liquids, undiluted by distance or dissipation in air or earth.

And all these conflicting emotions had come upon him in a moment, a few seconds at most: the sudden need to run from this place, or to lie down and sleep here, perhaps even to die here. And yet, paradoxically, he felt drawn to *be* here, in this small tree-shaded clearing with its horseshoe bower; but *irresistibly* drawn here, like an iron filing to a magnet. And while the Necroscope was so very tired—indeed deadly tired, of life itself—at the same time, incredibly, he found himself lusting after the young woman in the bramble bower, half-naked where the tree-thing's tendrils had reduced her clothing to ribbons.

"For God's sake, man!" Miller shouted, grabbing the Necroscope's arm, trying to haul him upright from where he'd gone to his knees in the soft loam. "Get it together, can't you, Harry? Don't you understand, man? This is what this damned thing does, and now it's doing it to you! But not to me, thank God, because for all that it's stronger than ever before, I'm at least partly immune. So snap out of it, Harry. I mean, surely you can see what's happening here?"

Harry's hands in the soil supported him, stopping him from falling on his side. Having understood what Miller had said, he fought what was happening, the invasion of alien poisons in his system; until in the next moment he was shocked awake—shocked into his five normal senses—when suddenly he felt the earth beginning to *move* under his hands!

Then, snatching himself back from the disturbance, he saw the sudden eruption of a cloud of soil and dusty leaf-mould, as emerging from below a leprous white, purple-veined rootlet shot up into view! Squirming to and fro, the stabiliser searched for something on which to anchor itself, which in turn caused Harry to cry his loathing out loud, stumble to his feet, and back off farther yet from the frantically lashing member.

But Greg Miller wasn't backing off; no, not at all. A puff of blue exhaust smoke and the sputtering, full-throated roar of his chain saw spoke however ineloquently of his intentions as he stepped up beside the Necroscope and swung the blade of the saw through inches of soil where the root humped and bulged. And he grunted his satisfaction as a three-foot length of the tentacle was severed, splashing its dark green and scarlet-tinged juices all about as it whipped like a crippled snake.

At which the *thing* itself—the bulk of the thing—went mad with pain and terror. Its "branches" shook as if in a hurricane; its towering, twenty-foot, wineglass-shaped mass lurched drunkenly this way and that; its lashing chitin-barbed tendrils were with-drawn and snatched up from the bower, twining in agony on high like the helix of some giant's DNA. And before the monstrous thing could regain control of itself:

"Now, Harry!" Miller shouted, finding another subterranean stabiliser rootlet and slashing it through in a shower of leafy debris. "The petrol, man! Use the petrol!" His meaning was very obvious.

As the Necroscope took up the plastic container, unscrewed its cap, ran under the thing's green canopy and set about drench-ing its bole, so the terrified lovers—bloodied, though not too badly, but wide-eyed in shock—came crawling in their rags from what was once their secret place. While beneath the creature's windmilling branchlike arms, Harry splashed the last few drops of fuel onto the dry leaf-mould at the foot of the thing, threw down the empty container and began to back away . . . until a franti-cally lashing branch buffeted him to the heaving earth.

Winded, dazed, and still feeling ill, Harry huddled there, and all about confusion reigned. But this close to the wounded, mad-dened thing, the deadspeak voices of its captive souls were that much louder in the Necroscope's metaphysical mind:

The primitive, uneducated voice of a hunter, a survivor of the last ice age, whose tribe had foraged these woods in a time when all the trees were ever-greens . . . the hoarse cries of a Beaker woman from 2000 B.C., taken from her hut where she lay heavy with child; and even the wailing of her unborn girl-child . . . a woad-daubed warrior, fatally wounded in a tribal feud and aban-doned, grabbed up by the ancient Thing before he could die a more natural death . . . a Celtic druid woman or Ollamh, who had actually worshipped the old monster before it killed her . . . young girls from local hamlets in a time when England lay under Roman occupation . . . and amongst these and many more, the sweet voice of a girl from the more recent past, whose name was Janet . . .

All of these lost ones, crying aloud their misery into the dead-speak aether . . .

If there was any cure, any antidote for the last dregs of the an-cient Thing's pheromone poisons that Harry's immune system was still working to repel, then this was surely it. For the Necroscope had never ignored the entreaties of the Great Majority, and he wasn't about to do so now.

Listen, he told the many captive souls, knowing that they finally heard his deadspeak. *I'm going to set you free. And if I can't . . . then I'll probably die trying, and join you anyway!*

"Harry!" Crouching down, Miller came swerving, zigzagging, somehow managing to avoid the old Thing's flailing branches as he swung his chain saw in a high arc, severing any that came too close. "Out of my way, Harry," he cried. "I'm going to set fire to this bastard thing!"

Holding the chain saw aloft in one hand, he fumbled in his pocket to find his cigarette lighter. But even as he found and brought it into view, so it was sent flying from his hand by a severed, frantically lashing tentacle and buried itself underfoot in the shuddering leaf-mould.

"God . . . *dammit!* Miller cursed, sobbing his frustration. Surrounded by flailing branches and tossing tendrils, he yelled: "Harry, find the lighter and use it. We have to put an end to this now, so *burn* the damn thing! Burn it to the ground!"

Down on his knees amongst twitching lengths of tendril and oozing branches as thick as his own arms, Harry groped deep in the quaking leaf-mould until at last he found Miller's lighter. But as yet more debris from the man's vengeful chain saw attack continued to rain down on him, the Necroscope saw something he would never forget—something which even he scarcely believed— that sickened him to his stomach. Some of the monster's dismembered, writhing limbs where they voided their fluids on the forest's slimy floor . . . some of them, indeed several of them, seemed coated or enclosed in sleeves of . . . of—

—But of what, *for God's sake?*

Harry saw that while one of these vilely spurting lengths was mainly blackened by time, its sheath wasn't so much bark as animal hide cicatrised and coloured with some kind of dark blue stain, forming a primitive, stylised pattern or tattoo image of a sharp-eared wolf!

But . . . *animal* hide? No, scarcely that, for in the Necroscope's unique mind he could even now hear the guttural "voice"—more properly the incorporeal thoughts or deadspeak—of the once owner of this grisly remnant:

You look upon my sigil, the voice said, *which I wore upon my forearm. For I am Gar Unkh who hunted the wild wolves. Alas that something hunted me also! But who is it who comes to free me? What, from the monster that seduced and killed not only me but likewise my fellow captives? I doubt that very much!*

Doubt all you like, Harry answered this voice out of time, *but that's the plan.* With which he thumbed the lighter's knurled wheel, saw blue sparks jump to ignite a strong yellow flame—

—Then let the burning lighter fall onto the fuel-soaked leaf-mould . . . and threw up an arm to shield his face when the earth beneath his feet seemed almost to explode!

"Out of there, Harry!" Greg Miller yelled in his ear, his hand on Harry's collar, dragging him from the sudden heat of a burgeoning inferno. "We can do no more."

But no sooner free of the flames, yanking himself from the other's grip, the Necroscope shouted back, "Yes we *can* do more! We need evidence, Greg!" And still retreating from the heat, he grabbed up some of the quivering members of the thing and half-carried, half-dragged them out from beneath the canopy to where he, Miller, and the terrified young lovers could stand in something of safety and experience the beginning of the end for the nightmarish thing:

The demented, agonised gyrations of its branches and tendrils as the fire began to consume them; the sputtering of its boiling juices and the morbid stench going up from them, which wasn't at all the usual smell of burning wood or green foliage; the hissing, piercing shrieks of pressured vapour jetting from the stumps of slumping members, so very much like screaming it might almost be an animal or perhaps even human sound. . . .

But as for the Necroscope: he was listening to something else.

Not to any imagined or fanciful death cry—nor even to the actual, harrowing, howling deadspeak of this evil, ancient thing—but to the glad, psychic voices of so many others. And all of these latter souls, the prisoners of a creature who had kept them and their voices to itself, pouring out their gratitude to this man they had never had the chance to know or even to hear of. But they would know of the Necroscope soon enough, now that they could join the Great Majority.

And as for the tree-thing:

Releasing its grip on these long-lost souls as finally it surrendered to the inevitable, the thing addressed the Necroscope directly in alien thoughts which only his deadspeak could translate or decipher:

You have killed me and all that would have sprung from me. No more shall I hear the sweet sad songs of them whose essences sustained me, whose spirits I in turn sustained within me. They flee me now, ungrateful, wretched things that they are.

To which the Necroscope replied: *They were simply victims at first, who you murdered. Then they were your captives, cold and afraid in the dark. Their "songs" were cries of terror, as I believe you know well enough.*

And the dying thing responded: *I wended these forest ways when your ancestors were savages. I have been here since times that even I cannot remember! So why have you killed me now?*

Because you're an ugly evil thing, the Necroscope replied, *whose time is over and done with in this and every other place.* And this last he said with authority, with absolute conviction, in the sure knowledge that there would be no room in any afterlife for such as this. For the Great Majority would never allow it.

The thing's members were shrivelling, its oily flesh burning, melting. It toppled towards the Necroscope, who retreated as a gaping, barb-lined mouth yawned at him through the stink, the smoke and flames. Close by, tinder-dry bushes were already on fire as, in one final orgasmic spasm, the thing opened sac-like sporangia in its trunk to eject a cloud of winged spores. With their flaccid rootlets dangling, the spores twirled in the air for mere moments before their fragile wings crumpled, sending them spiralling to the earth. Each as big as a man's thumb, pulpy and lifeless, already they were rotting.

Prodding one with his booted foot until it collapsed like a soggy puffball and sent up a vile stench, Greg Miller wrinkled his nose and grunted, *"Ugh!* Christ, what a God-awful mess!"

The Necroscope, and the trembling young couple where they clung to each other, all three of them could only agree. . . .

Muffled by the crackle and *whoosh!* of the fire, Constable Jack Forester's arrival had gone unheard, until a voice from behind the group of four snapped: "Greg Miller, you bloody crazy man! And Harry Keogh?" Then, as they turned to face him, the policeman also recognised the scratched and bloodied couple in their rags. "And you two?" he said. "Gloria Stafford and Alex Munroe, isn't it? Now what the hell . . . !?"

Behind the four the blaze was spreading. Wide-eyed, shaking his head in disbelief, the constable went on: "Miller, you mad bastard! Did you do this? What, are you trying to burn Hazeldene to the ground or something?" His voice hardened. "Or are you simply destroying evidence? Is that what it's all about?"

For to Forester it seemed that this part of the woods had been set on fire deliberately—which it had been, if not for the reason he'd proposed. But still it *seemed* that way to him—at least until a crippled, smouldering tendril came snaking out of the blaze, hooked itself onto his lower right leg and almost yanked his feet out from under him! Even as the constable cried out in shock and astonishment, however, trying instinctively to pull away, so the writhing tendril released him and shrivelled back into the inferno.

Shaken and staggering, completely off balance until Miller grabbed and steadied him, Forester looked again at the fire and saw blackened branches humping and vibrating where they burned: the involuntary, mindless activity of the ancient Thing's melting nervous system, or perhaps the expansion of internal fluids in the vicious heat. For the thing itself—or the central nest of ganglia that was or had been its alien brain—was most definitely dead.

The constable's lower jaw had fallen open. Closing it, he started to ask: "What in God's name . . . ?" But as his mouth dried up he shook his head and left the obvious question hanging—

—Until Greg Miller finished it for him. "*Nothing* in God's name!" he snarled, drawing Forester closer. "Nothing whatsoever to do with God, Jack. But now that you've seen it for yourself, surely you must see what it's got—and what it's *had*—to do with me? Or with *both* of us?"

Forester again shook his head . . . in denial, perhaps? But the Necroscope would have none of that. He showed the constable one of the severed "branches" which he'd dragged from the fire, the one with Gar Unkh's primitive wolf's head "tattoo" outlined in woad and the wartlike blemishes of self-mutilation, and kept as a trophy down through the ages by the ancient Thing. "So now you tell me, Jack," he said. "What do you make of this?"

As Forester's jaw fell open again, so Miller staggered and moaned, then stooped to take up into his trembling hands one of the other limbs that Harry had saved. And:

"*Look!*" he gasped, showing what he'd noticed to the constable. The Necroscope looked also, and at first saw nothing that meant anything to him—until the looks of understanding on the horrified faces of the two old enemies finally told the rest of the story, or more properly what remained of it.

"B-b-birthmark!" Forester stuttered, finding difficulty in getting the word out. But he was right: a raised, near-perfect, four-leafed clover design in dark red—a natural "blemish" or birthmark—was clearly visible on the scorched sleeve of preserved human skin that covered the severed limb.

"Janet's birthmark, yes," Miller confirmed the constable's observation in a hoarse whisper. "Inside her right calf, two or three inches below the knee."

"I know!" the policeman husked. "Janet was always self-conscious about that mark, even as a kid at school taking swimming lessons on Friday afternoons. I remember! Oh, I remember! I was in a class for older kids, but we all used the same pool on the same afternoon together. Poor Janet! She'd sit poolside, trying to hide that harmless little mark. Oh God! Oh God! As long as I can remember, I was always . . . was always . . ."

"You loved her, yes," Greg Miller sobbed. "But it was me—*I* was the one that Janet loved—and you've been making me pay for it ever since. Well that's all over and done with now! *Damn you, Jack Forester!*" Lashing out suddenly with a clenched fist, he knocked the policeman to the ground.

Touching a split, bleeding lip, Forester scrambled to his feet, shook his head to clear it, and mumbled, "Well, I suppose that after all you've suffered I had that one coming."

"That one and a lot more," Miller growled, closing on him.

But then the Necroscope stepped in. "That's enough. Now we should get the rest of these awful things into the fire." Turning quickly, he used his momentum to hurl the tendril with the prehistoric wolf hunter's sigil into the blaze.

"But that's evidence!" Forester at once protested.

"Of what?" said Miller. "Of your stupidity? The stupidity of all the people who called me a lunatic and convicted me? Do you really want to dig all of that up again? Me, I've had more than enough of that kind of limelight! I say Harry's right: we should finish this— all of it—right here and now."

"Cover it up, you mean?" Forester was doubtful. "After you spent all this time tracking it down? After what it's cost you? I don't understand."

"I did it for Janet," said Miller, his throat raw from the smoke and his broken sobbing. "I can move away from here, where no one knows me. I would have gone long ago, except I needed to do this first. And now . . . well, now it's done. But if you want to report this, well go on, go right ahead. And people will say you're even more crazy than I was—especially when there's no bloody evidence!"

Sobbing still, he spun around, hurling the branch with his lost love's birthmark into the heart of the fire. . . .

Harry spoke to Forester. "Is there a radio in your car?"

"Yes, of course." Again the policeman shook himself, as if he had just woken up.

"Then get back there and use it," said Harry. "Let's have a few fire engines out here before this gets completely out of control."

Forester nodded, headed back the way he'd come. But young Alex Munroe called out after him: "Hey, what about us?"

The policeman glanced at the trembling couple where they stood in their rags, daubed with dried blood and crisscrossed with cuts and scratches. They were fortunate that most of their injuries were minor, but still they needed attention. And turning to Harry, Forester asked: "Yes, what about them? I can call up an ambulance, of course, but then what?"

The Necroscope wasn't slow when it came to supplying quick answers and alibis. "They saw the blaze," he said, "and came to investigate. But they were caught between the fire and the brambles and got scratched up fighting their way out of the forest. Bramble thorns can rip your clothing right off your back. . . ."

And turning to the couple—or more properly to the girl—he asked: "Does that sound about right to you, miss? Or perhaps you'd prefer to let everyone know what you were really doing in the woods?"

She tilted her chin at him. "We're not ashamed of being in love, Mr. Keogh!" But then—glancing sideways at Alex Munroe, and seeing the way he nodded his head pointedly—she went on: "Still . . . your suggestion is probably for the best, er, Harry? And we're *very* glad you were here to save us a second time!"

Following which they found their way out of there into the cool clean air of the nearby fields. . . .

"What was that thing?" Munroe asked of no one in particular, as the five stood well back from the action, watching fire engines arriving and their crews scrambling to tackle the fire, a blaze that would yet go on to destroy more than two and a half acres.

"It was something alien," the Necroscope answered him. "It lured you into the forest, to a spot where it could do its evil work and remain unseen, unknown. It was a very ancient thing—as old as the hills and the last of its kind—a horror out of time that could either scare you off or draw you into its trap, then put you to sleep and kill you. Or maybe it would cause you to kill yourself!" With that last, he glanced knowingly at Jack Forester.

"Old Arnold Symonds?" The constable knew it was so.

"I think so, yes," said Harry.

Forester nodded. "And I might have been another victim. It doesn't bear thinking about."

And Greg Miller, far more in control of himself now, said: "I might have killed myself, too. Probably would have, except I think I was mainly immune to the monster's influence. It was my *hatred* kept me immune; I wasn't about to kill myself until I at least tried to kill it first! But you know, I think it may even have grown to recognise my presence? I felt it was playing some kind of game with me!"

Pointing at a near-distant vehicle kicking up dust along a dirt track, Gloria Stafford said, "I think that's the ambulance coming now."

And Harry asked her, "Have you two got your story right?"

Alex Munroe answered for both of them: "We were out walking, went to investigate a column of smoke in the woods and saw the fire. We panicked, stumbled into a large bramble patch, and so on and so forth."

"I'll never again feel safe in the shade of a tree," said the girl. "And I know that I'll always have nightmares."

"That goes for me too." Munroe put an arm around her, drew her close. "But when the nightmares come we'll always have each other." And she smiled at him, however wanly.

"That's it then," said Forester. "It's over."

Miller simply nodded, and Harry agreed, saying, "It would seem so, yes." And that was that . . .

———

. . . At least until the young lovers had been driven away, when it became plain there was that on Miller's mind which had been there for quite some time. For suddenly he turned to the Necroscope and asked: "Who are you, Harry? Not just your name but— I don't know—something else? I mean, who are you *really?*"

And Constable Jack Forester was quick to agree: "Yes, I've felt the same way about you ever since I first laid eyes on you dealing with that pair of local ne'er-do-wells. So who are you, Harry?"

"I'm nobody important," said the Necroscope. "I just know some things, that's all. You could say I feel things that other people don't. It's what I do. And sometimes it works out right, like this time. I mean, if I can help people, ease their minds, that's enough." *But more especially if they're dead people, who need all the breaks they can get and all they've got is me.*

But: "No," said Miller and Forester almost as one. And the policeman followed it up with: "I'm sure you're a lot more than that—but I'm damned if I can figure out what!"

And Greg Miller said, "I suppose we'll just have to let it go, like everything else that's happened today. But anyway, who or whatever you are, you have my thanks, Harry."

"Mine too," said the constable, nodding. . . .

When the Necroscope was on his own he spoke to his mother, who already knew much of what had happened. She'd heard it from the newcomers, of course, who were now firmly incorporated into the Great Majority.

That's a very wonderful thing that you've done, Harry, she said. *But you did put yourself in danger . . . again!* Harry could sense her incorporeal frown.

"You would have done the same, Ma," he told her. "You know you would, if you were able. And of course, we now know why you couldn't find any information on the girl: she just wasn't with you—she hadn't joined the Great Majority—couldn't, because she was trapped inside that thing along with all the others."

Still sensing his mother's frown, however, and before she could further upbraid him, the Necroscope quickly went on: "Ma, I won't argue with you; I'm simply asking after your newcomers, that's all. Because some of them were caught up with that creature for a very long time."

Yes they were, she replied, *and they suffered greatly. But the oldest of them—who should have moved on to higher places long ago—they have already caught up and passed on. Thanks to you, Son, all thanks to you.*

"Not all of it," Harry answered, shaking his head, humbled in the presence of his mother and the teeming dead. "I had help this time: Greg Miller. And anyway, I wasn't looking for praise, Ma."

Oh, we know you weren't, Son, she told him, but still her deadspeak "voice" was full of pride.

"What of the girl, Janet?" Harry inquired.

She's with her father now, the Necroscope's Ma replied. *We forgave him a long time ago for what he did, for he was in such pain, poor man. We frown on suicide, as you know; for if anyone knows how precious life is, it's surely the Great Majority! But we accepted him anyway. What else could we do? He was so . . . so disturbed. But now that they're together, we believe he'll be a lot better.*

Harry knew she would sense his nod when he said, "Yes, and it really wasn't his fault. Well, not entirely and probably not at all. Arnold Symonds was made to do what he did by that thing in the forest. You do understand that now, don't you?"

Indeed we do, she answered. *So you needn't any longer feel concerned, Son. Not about anything. All's well that ends well.*

And with that, feeling satisfied and fulfilled, the Necroscope nodded and went his lonely way. . . .

Harry and the Pirates

On this dreary mid-September day, Harry Keogh, Necroscope, was back in the graveyard in the old steelworking and ship-building town of Hartlepool, only seven or eight miles from the village on England's north-east coast where he had grown up in the care of a kindly aunt and uncle. However, to speak of Hartlepool in terms of steel and ships alone—terms more in keeping with an extinct but comparatively recent industrial past—while ignoring its rather more antique historical background, would be to do it an injustice. Indeed, for there's far more to this hoary old place than that.

In fact, in the town's most venerable quarter—in a small, weathered harbour lying leeward of the blustery spit that features as Hartlepool's most northerly point—the Necroscope had earlier talked to a Viking, a seafaring reaver who in his time had known the place as "Hjartapol." Known it, attacked it, and on several occasions even sacked it . . . but once too often.

Erik Haroldson—who was once called "Scarhelm" after the great white blaze of an axe gouge over his right eye—had told Harry:

Aye, and Scardaborg, too,—which Harry had understood to mean modern Scarborough—*and many another seaport along these shores, wherever we fancied were riches and fat juicy women! We raided 'em all! Why, the mere sight of a krakenship would cause panic: the wild flight of so many paleblood cowards that entire villages were deserted, left for us to sack! We were feared far and wide, from tip to toe of this entire eastern coast and even north of the Great Wall* [Hadrian's Wall]. *We raided around the northern point* [the Pentland Firth], *and south down the western flank as far as fair winds and our oars would take us. Hah! Did you think men called us "Varyargi"* [voyagers] *for nothing, Necroscope? We sailed wherever we desired to sail, and neither man nor scaly sea beast to say us nay!*

A boastful, swaggering speech that was quite obviously intended to impress. But:

"Well, evidently *someone* must have said you nay," Harry had answered him, and then deliberately yawned, "else I wouldn't be perched on this damp sea wall right now, bored nigh unto death, listening to your braggart's stories, while your drowned, crab-eaten bones lie buried in muck all of three fathoms deep in the harbour!"

This was very unusual for the Necroscope, who had obviously "got out of the wrong side of bed" this morning, as they say in those parts; for when conversing with the dead, Harry was normally the soul of compassion. Or perhaps it was just that he was weary and disillusioned. For in fact he was searching for someone—indeed two someones—one of whom he had loved, and one other he would have liked to know better and perhaps learned to love, but once again as so often before he'd failed to discover even the slightest trace of them. It was as if they had disappeared right out of this world.

As to why he'd searched here:

. . . Some years earlier Harry and his true love—his sweetheart from pre-teen times who had later become his wife—they had used to come here, walk all the way along the coal-streaked sandy shore from Harden to Old Hartlepool, then catch the coast road double-decker bus back home. Such a long walk might occupy an entire day, but it would also provide an opportunity to make love amongst the grass-topped sand-dunes; just such a lovemaking event as had got her pregnant. Then had come Harry's transition into the Necroscope—and into someone frightening, whom Brenda had considered a stranger—following which she and the infant had simply, or perhaps not so simply, gone away.

Now when time allowed Harry would search for her. Which was how he had ended up there, on the old harbour wall in that most ancient part of town: partly out of nostalgia but mainly in the hope—albeit a hope that was slowly but surely being eroded—that he might yet find something of Brenda and his son in these familiar haunts. No such luck, however, and on top of his disappointment the Necroscope had somehow got himself caught up in conversation with the long-dead, boastful, callous, and entirely unrepentant Viking Erik "Scarhelm" Haroldson.

His thoughts had been plainly "audible" to the dead Viking, of course—and to his crew, who had gone down with him—and Erik had been somewhat taken aback.

I had heard it rumoured that you were a friend of the dead, he'd growled in Harry's mind. *Yet here you mock my cold, watery grave and call me names! If I had life I do not think you would be so careless with your comments.*

"Bah!" the Necroscope had answered, scornfully. "If you and yours had lived your lives in this time, in my time, Erik, it's more than likely the gallows would have got you; or at the very least you'd be locked up for life! We don't any longer tolerate barbarians in my world, 'Scarhelm.'" Which wasn't entirely true or accurate; but in addition and for emphasis, Harry tossed his head and offered a deliberately scathing "*Huh!*"

Why . . . you . . . you! The Viking choked and spluttered while his crew roared with laughter, the same crew whose longship had gone up in flames beneath their feet, leaving them to jump over-board and drown, tangled up in the hurled, weighted nets of the town's brave fishermen; a dead crew, of course, who would never have dared to laugh at their chief in that bygone age when they had known life. And:

Damn you to hell, Necroscope! cried the Viking.

"And who knows?" Harry had answered. "Why, I might even end up there! But as for you, 'Scarhelm'—I know one or two things about death, and I can tell you this: it's unlikely such as you will ever get to see Valhalla! For after all, what were you for all your bluff and bluster? A pack of scurvy sea-wolves, that's all. A gang of blood-thirsty, cutthroat pirates!"

At which:

Ahhhh! A previously unheard voice had sighed in Harry's unique metaphysical mind, apparently in some distress. *But what a shame, Necroscope, that you'd call such as that one a "pirate." For if he is a pi-rate, what does that make me? Am I also out of favour, who have done and said nothin' hurtful to you? In which case a great shame indeed; for I am assured by a mutual acquaintance that, havin' been somethin' of a storyteller in your own right, you love a good tale. And indeed I have just such a tale to tell, that is if you don't mind talkin' to a "pirate." But a real pirate, mind you, or more prop-erly a privateer, remote not only in time but also in breedin' from the Viking scum who long since turned to slop in yon harbour's bilges.*

Eh? What's that you say? roared Erik Haroldson. For having heard something of what this unknown other had said through the Necroscope's mind, he felt doubly insulted. Moreover and worse, he sensed Harry's attention wandering away from him and knew it would be a while—if ever, or more likely never—before any living man would stop to talk to him again. Wherefore:

What? he continued to bluster. *Do you keep a dog to do your barking, Harry? And one with a "tale" to wag at that? Hah! Take my advice, Necroscope: curb this yappy pirate pup and listen to me. Aye, for I've many a tale of my own to tell—of the storm and the sea and the sacking of cities—and songs that will yet be sung in Valhalla! For as you can see, I have the kenning and use it well.*

But knowing that the Viking would sense the action, Harry shook his head. "You may have the kenning, Erik,"—meaning the style and poetry of the old Norse sagas—"but a bully's bluff and bluster is your real forte. And as for Valhalla: doesn't it puzzle you that you're not there yet? A thousand years gone by, and you're still here, stuck in the mud, unclaimed? It seems to me fairly obvi-ous: there isn't a single Valkyrie who would lend a hand to such as you. For while I'm sure that there were proud Vikings, some middling Vikings, and a few not so great Vikings, I'm also pretty sure that you must have been one of the poorest of them all! And I've no longer any interest in you."

With which he shut the furious Erik out and turned his attention to the newcomer, a self-confessed pirate whose deadspeak voice issued from a source some small distance away. "You said we had a mutual acquaintance?"

Oh, indeed! that one answered. *He offered advice on contactin' you, and explained how you had promised to return and talk to him from time to time. All I must do was wait until you were closer, he said, and then I too would be able to address you. I see now, however, that you've no time for fools, as witness the abrupt dismissal of the Viking. Well, that makes two of us, and I pray you will accept my word for it that I'm not wastin' your time.*

The Necroscope was intrigued. "And this mutual acquaintance told you I was . . . how did you put it, a storyteller?" Just for a moment Harry's eyes narrowed speculatively—then opened wide in sudden understanding. And finally he smiled.

"A-ha! And he also told you I'm a good listener, did he? In which case I think I know him. He was a serial womaniser in his own time, a seventeenth-century rakehell who related his sexual adventures to me so that I could write them up into a sensational novel, a so-called 'fictional' account. The son of an earl—and the black sheep of his family who eventually cast him out—his life was cut tragically short when an outraged husband shot him through the heart. But I never heard him complain about it; I get the feeling he thinks he got his just desserts! And taking into account certain of the things he's told me, so do I! Let's face it: he was hardly a pillar of the community, now was he? I mean, he was an utter scoundrel!"

Harry paused, and then—aware that the other was following his every word and action—shrugged before finishing off with: "But what the heck, we're friends for all that. . . ."

You have him dead to rights, Necroscope! said the other. *He was a likeable rogue, Henry Thomas Buckfast . . . even a scholar, however, er, debauched? That's if you'll permit a mere "pirate" an observation of that sort. Of disparate social origins, Henry and me, still we lived in the same era and lay dead in the same cemetery; that much at least we had in common, for which I know I shall miss him. . . .*

"What?" Suddenly the Necroscope was frowning. "What's that you say?" Surprise and dismay were apparent in a voice that the pirate "heard" as deadspeak, which frequently imparts much more than the spoken words. "You mention him in the past tense, saying you'll miss him? Isn't he any longer there, then? But wait!—we needn't talk across a distance like this—I know exactly where you are and can come to you."

Turning up his collar against rain that came suddenly, in a squall off the sea, the Necroscope climbed down from the weathered granite of the sea wall, hurried across the cobbled street and took cover under the arch of a recessed door in the wall of a centuried grey stone building. And without pause, all unseen, there he employed esoteric Möbius formulae to conjure a door of his own.

The transfer was instantaneous as he crossed the threshold, stepping from the harbour's dreary light into darkness absolute— that of the metaphysical Möbius Continuum—and out into the familiar co-ordinates of an almost equally dismal cemetery under cover of a buttressed pier in a high stone wall. It was a sorry place on days like this, this ancient graveyard that Harry knew so well, but—

—*Still and all,* he congratulated himself, however wryly, *at least it isn't raining!*

And so the Necroscope came to be in this place of so many memories: a host of them from his years of study at the technical college in the heart of the town, perhaps a mile away, and many more from his time—his far-too-short time—married to Brenda, when they'd lived together . . . just over there.

Moving out onto a pathway, he shook droplets from his coat, turned down its collar, looked up and over the wall, back across the street at the three-storied Victorian house where once he'd lived in the converted garret. He had enjoyed writing his short stories there in that tiny flat; or rather, writing the stories of . . . well, *other* people: tales they could no longer write for themselves. The stories of dead people, yes. Harry's friends . . .

He quickly drew back from that kind of morbid reverie. He'd had living friends, too. Well, a few. Jimmy Collins, from their school days in Harden Colliery—who remained a friend even now, and still very much alive at that—and Brenda, of course. Good old Jimmy was in Harden still, but as for Brenda and the child: their where-abouts remained a mystery.

And though this time Harry's thoughts were no longer of the morbid kind, again he pulled back from them. For reverie, nostal-gia, and wallowing in regrets—wondering where all the time and his youth had gone, and oh so quickly . . . *more* quickly than for most men, for his body was older than his mind—this kind of in-trospection wasn't like him at all.

No, it was simply that he was here again, so close to where it had all started. Here where his parapsychological powers had fi-nally matured, been mastered, and used during missions first of personal revenge, next in an outright war against the human spawn of monstrous beings from a world in a parallel universe: a world of vampires!

Since when . . . since when . . . he'd lost so *much!* Not least his wife and child. And yet . . . and *yet—*

—*Damn it to hell!*

For once again the Necroscope had shied from such memo-ries. And perhaps it was best that he shut them out. In just a day or two he'd be heading home again, to Edinburgh and his new love—or at least to someone he *hoped* he could love—because

117

despite that he was his own man for a lot of the time, for a great deal of it he was also Bonnie Jean's "wee man"! And B.J. had her way of—but how to say it?—of "retrieving" him, of calling him home at a moment's notice. Not to mention her *other* ways, which made Harry forget everything but her sweet mouth and body. . . .

So, if he was going to listen to this story that the pirate seemed so eager to tell him, he might as well do it now because there was no telling how long he would be here. First, however, he would prefer to get a little closer to his new contact among the Great Majority.

And so: "Pirate," he said. "Do you want to say something to me, let me know which plot is yours?"

I'm over here, Harry, said that one. And the Necroscope had no difficulty following his deadspeak instructions, the "sound" of the pirate's incorporeal voice, along rain-puddled paths and through rank upon rank of headstones—some fairly new but most of them old, lichened, and occasionally leaning—to a plot in a weed-grown corner whose only marker was a raised, badly chipped slab of mottled marble that bore no name, dates, or information of any sort. And:

"Pirate," said Harry. "I don't know if it was ever meant to be like this, but time hasn't done your resting place any great favours! No name and nothing else—not that I can see—not on this old slab."

My name? the other replied. *You'd like to know my name? I'd consider that an honour: to have the Necroscope callin' such as me by name! I'm Billy Browen, pronounced "Brown" without the e. To my shipmates I was Billy Brown of Penzance Town . . . that is, of course, among other things. They had a way with curse words, those old sea dogs!* And Harry sensed a throaty chuckle, despite that there was no longer a throat to issue it.

Billy Browen: Harry found the other's name oddly familiar. But no, it was simply that it rang so typically "piratical" in his ears (or more properly in his mind). And checking that the pirate's slab was dry and clean, using his overcoat tails for a cushion as he seated himself, he said: "You speak with a degree of authority—with intelligence, and not just that of a common sailor or swaggering pirate—

if you'll excuse the coarse negligence of my words. So that wouldn't by any chance be 'Captain' Billy Browen, would it?"

What, a Cap'n? Me? Billy's deadspeak conveyed his astonishment. *Now that's very flatterin', Harry, but it does elevate me above my station. For while I did have a little learnin' behind me, still I never made more than first mate—which was a deal better than deckhand; even a step or two up from Petty Officer—if such military soundin' rankings are applicable in respect of freebooters—but in any case and for all the alleged perks of secondary command, I wasn't much better off than a lackey or back-scratchin' personal watchdog to some of the worst Cap'ns a man ever served under! Oh yes, and just now and then to a handful of the very finest. Aye, for there's good 'uns and bad 'uns in every occupation, Necroscope, and that's includin' piracy. . . .*

Then after a pause, apparently curious in his own right, he continued: *So then, you took Billy Browen for a Cap'n, did you, Harry? What, like Henry Morgan, or Blackbeard, perhaps? Oh, and by the way, I served under canvas with both of 'em from time to time! Or maybe you were simply hintin' that you know a thing or two—this, that, and the other—about us buccaneers, eh?*

"Oh, I've known several pirates in my time," the Necroscope answered. "Or at least I've *heard* of them and even observed one or two at their work—or maybe I should say their art? And you know something, Billy Browen? It just so happens they were Captains all! Let's see now: off the top of my head there was Errol Flynn, who was known as 'Captain Blood.' And Burt Lancaster . . . he was of a purple hue, if memory serves. Then there was a very flamboyant Douglas Fairbanks Jnr. from . . . oh, from a *long* time ago, though not nearly as far back as you."

I never have heard of a single one of 'em! said Billy. *So I reckon you're right and I was well before their time.* And then, hearing the Necroscope's chuckle, and sensing the broad grin on his face: *But there, you're havin' me on, right?*

Harry could almost see the other's frown of disapproval and was instantly contrite. "Yes," he said, nodding. "But I'm truly sorry, Billy, if I appear to have taken advantage of your situation. I was just having a bit of fun, that's all. Those names I spouted: they were real men but unreal pirates. Just actors who played the parts of pirates for the entertainment of others. It was all costumes, ketchup, and plastic swords, if you see what I mean." And because his words were deadspeak he knew that indeed the other would "see" exactly what he meant, which he did. And:

Well bless my soul! Billy's amazement was made plain by the volume of his ethereal thoughts, momentarily lowered to no more than deadspeak whispers. *Who of my old gang would have believed it, eh? Movin' pictures larger than life, on canvases as big as mainsails! How things have changed . . . how they've moved on!*

"But not you, Billy," Harry answered quietly, thoughtfully. "And you know, there's a general rule about that sort of thing? I mean, how long dead people are required to linger down there: how long they wait it out in the ground, before they're allowed to—"

But: *Hey!* Billy cut in. *I was a pirate, Harry! As such I've done things I can't say I'm proud of . . . as part of a crew, you understand. But in the cut and thrust of things: well, it happens I was there! And never a plastic sword to mention, and damn few crushed tomatoes—er, ketchup?—either! So condemn me if you will, Necroscope, but that's who I am and that's the way it was. And anyway, let's face it, I have a long time to go before my years under this slab will equal the Viking Erik Haroldson's where he's soakin' in bilge, seaweed, and crab shit in yon harbour—if ever! Which I suspect is because there's bad 'uns and there's bad 'uns, of which I was by no means the worst!*

With a slow nod of his head the Necroscope allowed him that and said, "I'm not judging you, Billy. Who am I to do that anyway? Maybe I shouldn't have judged Scarhelm either; perhaps, in one way or another, the teeming dead judge themselves. It could be some kind of—I don't know—posthumous guilt thing? Maybe that's what kept my old friend Henry Thomas Buckfast down there all this time, because he knew he deserved it! But in any case, I'm glad for him; I'm glad to see he's finally moved on."

And now there's me, eh, Harry? And I've got tales of my own to tell. P'raps not as titillatin' as Mr. Buckfast's, but interestin', I can guarantee you that. And not a little dauntin', if you're of a delicate disposition, or your nerves aren't much to speak of. Not that that would apply to such as you, of course—not to a man whose forte lies in conversin' with corpses!

Harry nodded knowingly, perhaps even wonderingly, and said, "You're just dying to get something off your chest, aren't you, Billy?"

What, my "dead man's chest"? said the other with a chuckle. *Well of course! For who but a dead man can tell you the secrets of Davy Jones' locker, eh? And I'm just dyin' to tell them, am I? Well, so says Harry Keogh! But ah, no!* (A shake of an incorporeal head.) *I'm not dyin' to do anythin', not any longer. For dyin' is somethin' that men can do but once, and Billy Browen's already had his go!*

Following this up with a second deadspeak chuckle—however short-lived, before sensing his statement refuted in the Necro-scope's metaphysical mind, and at once recognising his perfectly understandable gaffe—the exanimate pirate corrected himself:

Er . . . by which I meant most men, of course! Most of us die but once. . . .

Then, after further gathering his ethereal thoughts: *As for wantin' to tell my story: p'raps it's somethin' like that guilt thing you were on about, which I'm tryin' to erase from my mind. For you see, it's not just some old bucca-neer's tall story I'll be relatin', Harry, but a truly strange mystery of the sea. And bein' as much involved as anyone, and moreso than most—havin' witnessed and been part of it from beginnin' to end—why, even down here in this forgotten grave of mine, still I can feel its echoes vibratin' down the decades! Which means that I'm as much a part of it as ever, for all that I never wanted to be. . . .*

And finally, after a shuddery pause of several seconds:

So yes, I would certainly like to "get it off my chest," as it were, and some-thin' of a weight off these bony old shoulders too. And if, as I've heard it said, a burden shared is a burden halved, then you'll be doin' me a service which I won't be forgettin' in a hurry. So then, if you'll just lend an ear, Harry, Billy Browen will be only too pleased to bend it for you.

Knowing the other could sense his every action, the Necro-scope smiled a wry smile and said, "Well, it seems you've got me hooked, Billy! Which I suspect you knew would be the case." And settling himself more comfortably on the pirate's slab, he contin-ued: "So since the sun has just come out, and I've an hour or so to spare, why don't I just sit here awhile and let you tell me your story, eh?"

Sensing the other's gratitude and perhaps his relief—despite that he tried to keep it and a sudden upsurge of eagerness hidden— the Necroscope shielded his own thoughts and wondered: *So then, does Billy have a secret agenda? Or is it just that he truly, badly desires to tell me his story and in so doing—as he's freely admitted—relieve himself of some personal guilt? As to what he might be feeling guilty about after all this time dead and buried . . . well, we'll just have to wait and see.*

But what difference did it make anyway? With the old pirate cold in his grave, safe beneath a fathom of centuried earth and wormy sod, what harm could there be in it?

And so: "Say on," said Harry. . . .

"The where and the when of it doesn't matter too much," Billy commenced his story, whose words sounded with such clarity in Harry's mind it was as if they were being spoken into his ear. "In fact, I've lain here so long that I'm no longer sure! It's entirely possible I'd confuse such particulars, aye! Anyway, I sailed with a Cap'n and crew under the Jolly Roger—the skull and crossbones, which marked us for what we were—and likewise under a tropical sun that glittered on an ocean calm as a millpond, where flyin' fish skipped over the ripples and there was just enough breeze to move the *Sea Witch* along, however slowly. 'Which' wasn't the vessel's name, you'll understand.

"As for the names of my fellows: well, in the main you must excuse my reticence, but old habits and a freebooter's vows die hard, Necroscope; I no more care to mention 'em to you here and now than I would then to some naval officer or hangin' judge in a court of law in London, Portsmouth, or Jamaica—not that I'm equatin' or associatin' you with such, you'll understand. But I can at least give my Cap'n a name—if not his real name—and thus make the story easier to tell and easier for you to listen to. So let's call him . . . oh, how about Black Jake Johnson, eh? I think that'll suffice, aye.

"Very well, the scene is set: with myself as the 2 I/C, and a crew of hardened pirates, all aboard Cap'n Jake Johnson's *Sea Witch* out there on that tropical sea on that very fine day.

"Up in the crow's-nest a mere squib of a lad had roped himself to the mast where he lolled half-asleep, and Cap'n Jake in his cabin countin' gold from our last venture, and all the rest of us doin' as little as possible. Which was when it happened.

"There came a whistle and a roar, and an eruption of ocean maybe four or five fathoms off the port bow. Strong enough that it rocked the ship, hurlin' spray up onto the deck and over the figurehead, it drenched me to my hide where I stood close in to the prow, holdin' fast to the rail. But what did it mean? What, a shot across our bows? It seemed the only possibility! We were currently at odds with the Royal Navy and certain other powers, of course, not to mention Black Jake's feudin' with a good many rival privateers, so the likelihood—which at first appeared a certainty—was that we'd been taken by surprise and were under attack!

"But up there in the crow's-nest young Will Moffat was wide awake by now, and already he was shoutin' down to us that there wasn't a single ship—neither friend nor foe—in sight. And scannin' the horizon all about on this exceptionally clear day, we could each and every one see that Will was absolutely right.

"Now, Black Jake was an intensely jealous man, who, trustin' no one but himself, always took his beloved mistress to sea with him. And she . . . well, truth to tell, Necroscope, I never in my life saw a more beautiful creature! Zhadia had somethin' of the Orient about her; also of the Americas—mainly South America, I suspect—and not forgettin' a touch of Spain. Just glancin' at her long, agile hands and slender fingers a man could almost hear the castanets. And her great, huge eyes: for all that they were oval, they were dark as some fiery Mexican woman's! As for her skin: it was of a colour so very slightly off white that it looked like cream and was almost as smooth; why, you could feel the warmth of the sun issuin' from her, and blazin' in the pure white bar of her smile. Except, of course, no man looked at her too close aboard Jake's *Sea*

Witch, for to do so could so easily bring the Cap'n's fury down on any admirer's or suspect ravisher's head. Keelhaulin' a man was only the least of Black Jake's punishments; while a more permanent option might be to rope him to the anchor, and sink him five fathoms deep! For which reason Zhadia was mainly confined to their cabin.

"But on days like this with a sky so blue, the breeze blowin' gentle in the sails, and the ocean clean as a whistle, with never a sign of friend or foe on its broad smilin' face, why, it would have been a crime to keep her locked away; at which times she doubtless prevailed upon Jake for a breath of fresh air and a taste of salt sea waft, if only for a little while. Which was also when Jake, ever busy with his charts and his gold-countin' obsession and such, would task me, his faithful Mr. Browen—or just "Mister," as he was wont to call me—to ensure no scurvy dog came sniffin' or castin' a licentious eye on Jake's darlin' Zhadia.

"Which in turn sets the scene for that day of the whistlin' roar and the waterspout that drenched me and the girl both; for she was right there in the prow, her hair blowin' in the breeze and her figure outlined like some young goddess where her dress pressed to her like a lover . . . except it was never my place to say things like that, nor even to think them! But it *was* my job to see to her security; which is why I grabbed her up where she swayed with the ship's rockin' motion, and held her fast so she wasn't swept overboard. And in the next moment:

"'Hands off her, you lecherous lout!' Who but himself, Black Jake Johnson, come out on the deck, his legs braced, meaty fists clenched, and dark eyes aglint where they drilled into mine! And stridin' on legs like pillars so in tune with the motion of the sea that you couldn't knock him down with a cannon shot—with his hand reachin' for his cutlass, all menacin' like—he came scowlin' and snarlin' in my direction!

"Well, struck dumb in the confusion of the moment, there was I thinkin': *Billy, my son, innocent as you most definitely are, still you're surely doomed!*

124

"Until in the very *next* moment, as the ship swayed yet again on the settlin' swell, finally I found my voice:

"'Now then, Cap'n darlin',' says I, releasin' Zhadia, 'just you hear me out! It appears we were fired upon—a shot across our bows that came so close it rocked the ship and drenched the foredeck, which disturbance you must surely have noted for yourself. And with regard to the woman: I was only doin' my duty as I saw it, as ordered by my master, which is to say you, Cap'n.'

"Black Jake took in what I'd said—a shot across our bows, the *Sea Witch* under attack!—and his narrow eyes opened wide. 'Every man to his station!' he roared. 'Ready the damn cannons! What? Damn ye—have ye all lost what little sense ye had?' And stompin' to the rail he called up to the lookout, 'Ho there, in the crow's-nest! Where's the bloody enemy?'

"And up there in the nest, Will Moffat, all seventeen years of him—wide awake now and scannin' port, then starboard, this way and that through a glass, until finally somethin' tells him to look up—eventually callin' down, 'Nary a vessel in sight, Cap'n, sir! And anyway, that weren't a cannonball but somethin' that fell from the sky!'

"'*What!*' yells Black Jake. 'Why ye—'

"'Look on high, quick!' Will shouts back. 'Why, you can see the trail it left!'

"Cranin' our necks, we all of us looked and saw this spiral of yellow smoke gradually meltin' away. And nothin' else but an odd smell like burnin' tar, and a sky full of blindin' blue all the way to the horizon.

"Then Zhadia, havin' climbed up to the quarterdeck, callin' down to the Cap'n, 'Jake, I see it! It's in the water, driftin' there but fallin' behind. Gold in the sea, Jake, and a glory to behold!'

"'What's that?' he calls out to her. 'Gold, did ye say? Are ye daft, woman? Gold don't float!'

"But without lookin' back at him, her voice barely audible, and with her huge eyes fixed on the water astern, she sighs and answers, 'Gold in its colour, Jake! In its lovely colour. And I wants it, oh, how I *wants* it—this cloth of gold, or cloak of gold, whatever it be may be—a-floatin' there on the sea! Will you not catch it up out of the water for me, Jake?'

"By which time he'd joined her on the quarterdeck and could see what she was on about. And: 'By God!' he swore—but so low it went almost unheard, under his breath, as it were: a singular circumstance where Black Jake was concerned—'But that's a fine bit of . . . well, whatever it is!'

"Also at which time, the gentlin' sea breeze had fallen completely away, so that the sails hung slack from the yards. Jake saw that we were becalmed, and there was Zhadia clingin' to his arm and pointin' at the thing in the sea where it lolled on the last few ripples of its arrival. But still—bein' an obstinate man and not wantin' to appear at Zhadia's beck and call—Jake stroked his beard and spoke up loud, givin' himself a reason to retrieve the thing in the water:

"'Cloth of gold? P'raps and p'raps not. But haven't I heard it said that when lightnin' strikes a sperm whale it causes the beast to throw up this rare, valuable spume from its gut? Ambergris, it's called; sometimes it's grey as ashes and other times yellow as gold. Well, whatever, I'd be a fool to pass it up. So lower the boat, damn ye, and snap to it!'

"And so the thing was brought aboard. . . .

"Now note if you will, Harry: I say 'thing,' the reason for which will become clear as I proceed. For now, however, if only for a moment, let me pause to collect my thoughts. A story like this, it needs to be told with special care. The end must astonish; it should come suddenly—as a revelation!—sufficient to startle and even *shock* the unsuspectin' mind . . . !

"Er—but not the Necroscope's mind, eh? Not the mind of a man who has seen things sufficient to shock other men rigid and frighten them into early graves—and then *talk* to them there! A man with such powers that . . . that . . .

"But there, we understand each other and you know my meanin'.

And so I'll need but a moment to arrange the way my tale's to be told.

"Will you grant me that much, Harry? Good!"

While the dead pirate composed himself, or more properly, while he composed his story, the Necroscope was given to ask himself: "Just what am I doing here?" But then again, what else would he be doing if not this? Because the fact was that recently, if he wasn't searching for his wife and child, or answering the calls of the dead, consoling them wherever possible, then he was just as likely to be answering someone else's call—indeed, *rushing* to answer it and helpless to stop himself!—B. J. Mirlu's call, that is, from her wine-bar seat in Edinburgh. Bonnie Jean, yes, Harry's new love; but a strange love that as yet he wasn't sure of. The circumstances of their affair were peculiar and confusing to say the very least, and the Necroscope's thought processes were even more confused whenever B. J. featured in them. She was an extremely fascinating woman.

Fascinating but strange, yes . . .

Well, and what else was new? It seemed as much Harry's lot to stumble across weird situations and strange characters as it was for someone who was accident prone to trip over cracked paving slabs or hammer his thumb while nailing down a loose floorboard—*and* hit a water pipe! And what was Billy Browen if not another of that curious ilk: a somewhat odd and, on this occasion as on so many others, a very long-dead person?

But likeable? Plausible? Harmless? Well, so far so good. . . .

Frowning—but keeping both the frown and his thoughts to himself—the Necroscope found himself considering the quality of Billy's deadspeak; not his vocabulary or way with words, but more properly the "sound" of the pirate's incorporeal thoughts. Also, along with this unusual resonance (previously noted, when the dead man's words had rung with such clarity in Harry's mind it was as if they'd actually been spoken in his ear) certain of Billy's deadspeak's concepts had registered as incongruous with the Necroscope. For instance those names which he had so easily—and mistakenly, or possibly even falsely?—dropped. Such as when he'd placed Sir Henry Morgan alongside the infamous Blackbeard . . . strange bedfellows indeed, those two! And in addition he'd then boasted of how he'd sailed under both of them! Or was that all it had been? A typical, piratical flourish of no great consequence: quite simply a boast.

For over and above the silver screen idols Harry had joked about, he did in fact know one or two more things about pirates than he'd so far admitted; as a pre-teenager he had been fascinated by their storybook adventures. If memory served, Sir Henry Morgan had been—initially at least—some sort of gentleman privateer rather than a pirate proper, and for a time he'd even been Governor of Jamaica! Whereas Edward Teach, or "Blackbeard" as he'd been known . . . well *he* had been something else! Nothing less than a monster!

And again the Necroscope was given to wonder about Billy's boast. Was it really possible that he'd sailed under *both* captains? Had they been contemporaries then? If so, that wasn't the way Harry remembered it from his pre-teen reading. Henry Morgan had died of his excesses—"dropsy" or oedema brought on by his gorging and the massive drinking bouts that had got him suspended as a drunk from his duties as, of all things, a judge!—at Port Royal, Jamaica, sometime in the 1680s. While, on the other hand, Edward Teach had only commenced his pirating in the first quarter of the eighteenth century. Thus there could easily be a difference of forty or more years between Morgan's and Blackbeard's buccaneering. Or, if Harry based his calculations on the opposite extremes of those dates as he seemed to remember them—dates which might well be inaccurate—then the variance could be as little as twenty or twenty-five years; but even so Billy's claim would only just fall within the realms of possibility.

As for the variance in the natures of this pair of legendary figures—so pronounced that they had been literally poles apart—the Necroscope couldn't help but wonder at the changes Billy Browen must have experienced serving first under "officer and gentleman" privateer Sir Henry Morgan, then under the blood-lusting pirate Edward Teach. Teach had been known to prostitute his own wives—at least twelve or thirteen of them, in almost as many ports of call—to members of his crew, and to torture in various "games of endurance" those selfsame crewmen!

So then, in the main they'd been as different as chalk and cheese, this pair of freebooters. But there again, hadn't Billy made mention of going to sea with "some of the worst captains a man ever served under—and now and then with a handful of the very finest . . ."? Indeed he had, and so for the time being Harry put his doubts and suspicions aside.

All of which had passed through Harry's unique mind in far less time than it takes to tell, and all of it shielded so that no other person—alive *or* dead—could have acquired or in any way intuited his thoughts.

And yet . . . there was this low, almost "inaudible" buzzing in his mind; inaudible because of course it wouldn't be audible to anyone but Harry. It was similar to the interference between active, disparate electrical gadgets when they are brought into close proximity: a kind of static. Or maybe the hum of a record-player's speakers when there's no disc on the turntable and the volume is turned up way too high.

Yes, that could well be it: as if during this conversation between Harry and the pirate, the psychic aether's "volume" had suddenly been turned all the way up. But if so, by whom and for what reason?

Or perhaps it was just another manifestation of the Necroscope's burgeoning parapsychological powers, of which as yet he had grasped only the most basic ground rules. For example—and despite certain baffling and enigmatic statements by no less an authority than Albert Einstein—Harry still believed that the past, the present, and the future were three entirely different concepts. For there were things about the Möbius Continuum that he hadn't as yet discovered . . .

It was now well into the afternoon towards evening, and drifting in from the east the clouds had cloaked the ancient cemetery in gloom. It was beginning to look like rain again, and the Necroscope had had quite enough of that for one day. Also, his backside was feeling the cold even through the material of his coattails, and his knees were gradually stiffening up. Harry wasn't used to it; for all his powers he was only human, and following a recent metamorphosis—more properly a metempsychosis—his physical body, while in good shape, was nevertheless many years older than his metaphysical mind.

And so: "Better get on with the story, Billy," he prompted the pirate, who had been silent for some time now. "It'll start to get dark in the next hour or so, and if it rains I'll look a complete fool sitting here in the downpour!" Not that that last was ever going to happen; it was just a figure of speech. If he so desired, Harry could take the Möbius route out of the cemetery before the fall of the second raindrop!

Ah, the darkness, of course! said Billy. *You wouldn't care to be sittin' there on my cold, cold marker in the dark of night. Absolutely not! But you see, Harry, where I am, I've long since stopped considerin' such concepts as daylight, moonlight, starlight and such. For down here in the ground there's no light at all! None whatsoever! And there's no warmth, either—or there wasn't, until you came along. . . .*

And along with that last, once again the pirate's throaty, deadspeak chuckle. Which had the Necroscope wondering (but only to himself): *Is there perhaps something a little too eager, too cunning and lustful, about that chuckle of his? Or is it simply the low, guttural laughter of a villainous old seafarer? And if the latter, just how villainous was he . . . and is he still?*

But then, as if in denial of Harry's inward-directed suspicions: *So there you go,* said Billy Browen. *It wasn't ignorance or lack of respect on my part, that would have seen you sittin' up there in the dark and the damp, but simply my forgetfulness. After all these many decades of earth and worms—and of bein' bodiless, of course—it had slipped my mind how the livin' are accustomed to the natural comforts of a fully fleshed existence. And with the sort of mobility that you command, Harry, why, it's hardly surprisin' that you won't allow the mere elements to inconvenience you. . . .* and following a moment's pause, but far more quietly now: *So, how long do we have then?*

Glancing at the eastern sky—framing a darkly oppressive seething of clouds within a stormy, angry tossing of the higher branches of nearby trees—Harry passed that image down to the pirate in his grave. And: "Not very long," he said. "Perhaps an hour? And then I think the darkness and the damp will arrive at about the same time. Which is when I'll be leaving."

But now that we've met, as it were, we can still talk even at a distance . . . is it not so? It felt like Billy was grasping at straws.

"We could," Harry replied, "but I prefer not to. You won't find me shouting across the room at my friends. When I speak to someone like this I want it to be up close and personal; I like to think they're not just bones or dust, but that they're there in body as well as mind—even though I know they can't be and aren't."

He sensed the other's incorporeal nod, his disappointment. *So then,* said Billy, *it appears I'm not goin' to get it told in one visit. Not all of it, anyway. And while I know your time is precious, still that's a shame.*

"But you can at least get *something* more of it told," said the Necroscope. "And after all, it's not as if you'll never get finished with it, now is it? For like you've said: this is just one visit, right?"

What? The pirate's astonishment was almost tangible. Likewise his relief, the deadspeak sigh which he made no attempt to suppress as he gasped: *Are you sayin' you'll return? Well then, now I know for sure why the dead are so taken with you. For you really are their champion—yes, even a dead pirate's champion—aren't you, Harry Keogh?*

Trying to hide his embarrassment behind a second glance at the darkening sky, and failing, Harry answered, "I can feel the wind coming up, Billy. And by now the waves in Old Hartlepool's harbour will be moving Scarhelm Haroldson's bones around a bit. It looks like it may rain a lot sooner than I thought. So then, will you continue your story, or shall we call it a day—or a night, whichever?"

I'll continue, of course! said Billy Browen at once. *And I thank you once again, Necroscope, for affordin' me the opportunity to relieve myself of somethin' of the weight of this thing. For who else but you among the livin' could ever hear the story out and perhaps even appreciate its horror, eh?*

And as Harry eased his joints a little, again shifting his backside's position on the other's unmarked marker, he couldn't help but notice how the volume on the deadspeak aether had been turned up one notch higher still. . . .

"The thing from the sea, but more properly from the sky," Billy recommenced the telling of his story, "that cloth-of-gold *stuff* that was no more lightnin'-struck sperm whale puke than I'm the Lord Mayor of London—that shimmerin' shawl or dress spun from the cold glow in the heart of some weird, unearthly treasure—had been plucked from the sea and brought aboard the *Sea Witch;* 'which' was when our troubles began.

"Zhadia wanted possession of it immediately. She was hypnotised by its glitter, how dazzlin'ly it reflected the sunlight; and the fantasy of its featherweight fragility: the way it wove and wafted in the slightest puff of air where the crewmen who'd lifted it from the water hung it from the riggin' to dry. Amazin'ly, it seemed *already* dry, and no more than five minutes out of the sea; with salty white crystals driftin' down off it onto the deck as soon as they formed, because they couldn't cling to the sheerness of its weave! By 'sheerness' I mean its incorruptible oneness, its purity—or maybe its utterly corrupt *im*purity?—which wouldn't permit of any familiarity or mixin' with lesser 'elements'; by which I mean *inanimate* elements. . . .

"Well, leavin' off from what they ought to have been doin',

one by one the crewmen sidled up scratchin' their chins to look at this . . . but this what? This raiment? This lump of sky-stuff that seemed made out of sunlight? This gold-shimmerin' wisp, as light as a fairy's fart? A nigh weightless thing, aye, that yet had enough of weight to cause it to plummet into the ocean like it was shot from some heavenly cannon!

"And for a while Black Jake Johnson, who was as much taken with this wonder as anyone else, simply stood there and allowed these casual inspections. Until, snappin' out of it, he yelled, 'Ho, there, Missus!' (his 'pet' name for Zhadia). 'What's this, then? Will ye stand there gawpin' the live-long day, like these monkey-boys who seem to believe they're crewmen—in which case they should be about their duties earnin' a dishonest doubloon, *instead of standin' here scratchin' their hairy backsides*!

"Which was more than enough to send them off about their work, though not without many an oddly wistful backward glance, as Jake took Zhadia's arm and gentled her belowdecks away from that thing hangin' so limp in the riggin'. Limp now, aye, as if it had quit attemptin' to float free of the ship on the slightest waft; which could be because there wasn't any longer even a stir of air, we were that becalmed.

"As for the thing's rich glitter: it seemed to have burned itself out now, so that dull patches were showin' through, like the sides of a fish where his scales have gone missin'. Or maybe it was just the evenin' light, fallin' on the sky-cloth from a different angle as the sun dipped down towards the horizon.

"Sky-cloth, aye, that's how I first thought of it: as somethin' woven in the full of the moon, whose golden light had got caught up in it. *Hah!* First impressions and all. Which as often as not will lead a man astray. By which I mean that the thing's burnin' yellow aspect might as easily have been a reflection of hell's molten sulphur as the light of moon- or sun-beams!

"And so the night came on, and the stars so bright and the sea so still. . . ."

———

"It was a peg-leg called Pete—(no, I'm not kiddin'!)—who was standin' watch that night. Stumpy Pete Parsons, aye, whose left leg from the knee down had been eaten by a hungry shark when he fell in the sea while hangin' his arse overboard to do his business. Pete's footfalls betrayed his identity each time he went on patrol; or rather one footfall, followed by the thump of his mahogany fittin'! In the heat of many a tropical night, sweatin' blood in a hammock belowdecks—or up in the cool of the still night air, on those rare occasions when Black Jake would permit it, when it was too hot even for him, the hell-spawned devil—I'd hear Stumpy Pete Parsons comin', hummin' some sea shanty or other while keepin' time with the slap-*thump!* slap-*thump!* slap-*thump!* of his approach.

"This wasn't one of those rare, up-top nights such as I've mentioned, however; in fact it was singularly cool belowdecks, where the gentle lappin' of the sea and the occasional creakin' of the ship's oaken ribs—and Pete's monotonous, echoin', slap *thump!* overhead patrollin', of course—all combined, were like some lovin' mother's lullaby, puttin' me and doubtless the rest of that weary crew to sleep.

"Only once in the dead of night did I come awake, thinkin' to hear a thin, quaverin' cry . . . most likely that of some seabird, grateful for a yard-arm to light upon. So I thought while slippin' back into sleep: the cry of a seabird, aye—

"—Except I was wrong and it wasn't!"

"Black Jake Johnson's orders for that night had been simple indeed. 'Stumpy Pete, ye old peg-leg,' he'd said, 'in a calm such as this 'un, ye may *think* that no one's likely to come creepin' up on us. And so ye may also *think* that keepin' watch is hardly necessary . . . but it is! Ye'll keep the lanterns lit, both fore and aft; ye'll keep the rats from the galley, the old *Sea Witch* from sinkin', and yereself off the rum, of which everyone knows ye're too damn fond! Now, have I said enough?'

"'Aye, Cap'n,' says Pete, with a snappy salute.

"'Also,' Jake goes on, 'should a wind come up—or even a breeze to stir the sails—ye'll wake me first, then the rest. Is it understood?'

"'Aye, aye, Cap'n!' Another salute, and that was that.

"But the next mornin', as dawn broke, its pale light filterin' through a knothole in the strakes, a wind did indeed come up. The first I knew of it was when the ship groaned and leaned over to leeward a little as a risin' wind caught us side-on. It was no big blow—no tropical storm, as it were—but enough to swing my hammock about a bit until I sensed the motion.

"But what was this? No cursin' from Black Jake Johnson? No hollerin' or blasphemin', which there must surely be if he were up and about while all the rest slept on? Ah! But no sooner the thought than the Cap'n's bull roar:

"'Where is he? Where's that peg-leg, Stumpy Pete Parsons? For as Davy Jones is my witness, I'll have his mahogany fittin' sharpened to a point and relocated so good and tight that he'll never sit down on the job again! No, nor anywhere *else* for that matter! Where are ye, ye idle old sea slug!'

"Fearin' Jake's righteous rage, the rest of the crew were quick from their rest, and I give myself credit that I was just as quick and quicker. Not yet wholly or decently dressed, there I was at the helm, fumblin' with my buttons and toggles, and at the same time swingin' the *Sea Witch*'s prow leeward to help her stop fightin' the anchor, which I believed had got caught up on the bottom.

"Meanwhile the wind had come on stronger; young Will Moffat was monkeyin' up the mainmast to the crow's-nest; the crew were about their accustomed duties, those who had such, and the rest were waitin' on Black Jake's instructions. Which was when someone stumbled across Stumpy Pete Parsons. Except that someone—whose name isn't important, and in any case I can't remember it—wouldn't have known it was Stumpy Pete at all if his peg-leg hadn't been stickin' out of the wizened bundle of rags that lay there on the deck: a varnished hardwood limb that rolled free of the loose fittin's on Pete's shrivelled leathery stump when the deckhand who'd found him nudged it with the toe of his boot!

"Well, even Black Jake was dumbstruck when the ship's sawbones (he'd been a landlubber who'd run off to sea when several of his patients died from his remedies) unwrapped what was left of poor Pete from clothes as brittle as beached, sun-dried seaweed. Only six or seven hours ago this had been a man, albeit a one-legged man, of firm flesh, a sound heart, a full blue beard of which he was proud and a healthy appetite. Yet now—

"—Stumpy Pete was dead as a doornail, a thing of skin and bones, a veritable husk! His eyes were open but glassy, frozen in some nameless horror; his mouth gaped in a frame of fretted lips, where one or two stained fangs leaned like weathered old tombstones in the dark of that last long yawn; his cheeks were sunken in, as if his final act had been to suck air for a *second* scream (perhaps because the *first* one had come out a thin, quaverin' squawk much like a seabird might make?) and his once-proud beard had been reduced to patchy stubble that the risin' wind was liftin' from his parchment face and chin like so much dust!

"Well, to give Black Jake credit, he made a quick recovery from whatever shock or astonishment he might have felt; in less time than it takes to tell he was up on the after deck shoutin' over the howlin' wind: 'What, are ye not only blind but stupid, the lot of ye? The cable's taut and the vessel strainin' like a bloodhound on its leash. So slip the anchor, says I, before the *Sea Witch* suffers an injury! Jump to it, ye godless lot! And as for this blow': we'll go wherever the wind takes us and let the old ship ride it out!'

"Then he joined me at the helm, and said: 'Well, Mister. I see you were up and about at least . . . or anyways pretty quick. So then, what d'ye make of all this? I mean Stumpy Pete Parsons bein' dead and all; that and the way of it. Is this a rum to-do or what, and did ye ever see its like before?'

"'Well truth to tell, Cap'n Jake,' says I, 'there's no end of things here that I never saw or heard of before. . . .

"'Well then,' says Jake, 'say on, Mister, say on!'

"'First off,' says I, 'about lightnin', sperm whales, and what some say is regurgitated in certain strange circumstances. Now then, I've never in my life heard anythin'—'

"'Now you hold fire there, Mister!' the Cap'n cuts me off, scowls, and quickly goes on to say: 'Oh, I know what ye're gettin' at, aye.' But then he chuckles—somethin' *mighty* rare to hear!—and says, 'My ambergris story, eh?'

"'Well, Cap'n,' says I, 'I do know a little somethin' about ambergris, but as for lightnin'-struck whales, I—'

"'A yarn made up on the spur of the moment,' says he, cuttin' me off again. 'There I was: Zhadia wailin' for me to fetch that cloak, dress, or whatever aboard the old *Sea Witch*, and me bein' unwillin' to oblige her—or rather, unwillin' to be *seen* obligin' her! What, Black Jake Johnson hastenin' to the beck of a mere female—even one as rare as this 'un? Why, if certain of the scum aboard this ship should see that kind of weakness in a man—or *any* kind of weakness, for that matter—the next thing ye know . . . But there, Mister. I'm sure ye get my drift. So then, that's that and then there's the other. In the main it was Pete Parsons I was enquirin' of; Pete, and what ye might make of the way of his demise?'

"'Aye,' I offer a thoughtful nod. 'Which is where I say we should begin at the beginnin'.'

"'Eh?' says Black Jake, frownin'. 'Explain.'

"And so I did. 'It started when that thing fell out of the sky: that splash of queer brilliance, like an oddment left over from a bolt of heavenly—or hellish—golden weave.'

"'A bolt?' says the Cap'n, tweakin' my meanin'. 'Aye, like a bolt from the blue, eh?'

"'But no simple shootin' star such as we've seen on many a night,' says I. 'No, not this thing that comes spiralin' down, landin' with a force that rocks the ship, then ends up floatin' all serene on the sea until we bring it on board and hang it in the riggin' . . . which is when the weird of it begins. You saw it for yourself for sure, Cap'n. In your woman's eyes: the lustin' after it! And not only Zhadia—with a pretty woman's need for pretty things—but the crew, too. Not one of them could resist it but must come and ogle the thing, fascinated by it as though it were some *real* treasure and not just a scrap of some strange golden fabric fashioned in the stars.'

"'A fascination, aye!' Jake husked. 'And for a fact I felt it myself: the queer pull of it. So much so that I was quick to remove Zhadia from its lure. I can't say why, but I didn't want her touchin' it, that's all. . . .'

"Now not too long ago the Cap'n had spoken of weakness 'of any kind' (for which read fear,) and of his stubborn refusal to display such. Yet I had long known Jake to be not only a shrewd and vigilant man but somethin' of a superstitious one, too. And it seemed to me as we stood there at the helm that for once his cagey, suspicious nature had surrendered to his credulous side. It had been, however, but a momentary surrender. And now—

"—Suddenly pullin' himself together, he searched my face with a penetratin' gaze, and snapped: 'Oh, and what of ye, *Mister?* Didn't ye feel it too? Or is Cap'n Jake just an old softy, eh? P'raps soft in the head, ye know?'

"'What, you, soft in your head, Black Jake Johnson?' says I at once. 'No, never! Not a bit of it! Oh, I *felt* it, Cap'n! But sharin' your own keen interest in such remarkable occurrences—which is all you're feelin', I'm certain sure, a consumin' interest not only in nature but also in the *un*natural, and nothin' to be afeared or ashamed of in that—and bein' much like yourself attracted but resistant to idle fancies and such, why—'

"'Enough!' says Jake. 'None of yere poxy flattery, Mister! Just tell me what ye think happened here, and quick about it.'

"'Well you heard what the sawbones said, Cap'n Jake,' says I. 'How Stumpy Pete would have lived a lot longer if he'd liked apples as well as he liked rum. A bad case of scurvy is what it was; the worst case ever, which caught up with Pete very sudden like. *Very sudden, aye.* Scurvy, Cap'n! Or at least, that's what the sawbones says.'

"And in a while, starin' through thoughtful, narrowed eyes far across the ruffled sea, Jake slowly nods and says: 'Scurvy, ye say? Well, p'raps, Mister. But I'm sure ye must have noticed where the peg-leg was found, lyin' stiff as a board on the deck? Directly under that thing hangin' in the riggin', that's where! And do ye recall yestereve, how it was grown a mite dull? Well, just look at it now, will ye.' He nods again, seemingly directin' my gaze fore and amidships.

"But before I can look proper, the Cap'n catches my elbow and says, 'Listen, Mister. Ye started off talkin' about weirdness and things ye never saw nor heard of before. Well, I have to agree there's somethin' weird here. In fact I'd have the men jettison yon thing—a shroud for Peg-leg Pete in the dampness of the deeps, which is where that poor bugger's bound—except I fancy it may have some real value; and anyway I won't be seen to be the least bit leery of it. Hell's teeth, I'm *not* leery of it—nor anythin' else, for that matter!—but this so-called "pirates crew" of mine just might be. So no more talk of weirdness, ghosties, ghoulies, and such. The peg-leg's no great loss, truth be told, but we don't want anyone else jumpin' ship. Now ye'd best hurry on down and chivvy that bunch of gawpin' fools up a bit, get them workin' again, attendin' to the *Sea Witch*'s welfare, before their lazy feet take root in the plankin'! Off ye go.'

"Havin' said his all, and with another nod amidships—his eyes reflectin' a certain golden glimmer—Black Jake let go my elbow and shoved me in that direction. So off I went, down onto the deck amidships, fightin' the blow along the way.

"And there it was, with a handful of crewmen just standin' there, starin' up at it where it whipped in the wind. Except it didn't really whip and snap, not like a sail's canvas, but sort of floated there all languid like despite the rush and bluster. As for yestereve's dullness, as remarked upon by the Cap'n: not any longer. Because for all that the day was overcast and spray flyin' from a surgin' prow, that sky-cloth shone like burnished metal: for a fact, like precious gold!

"Indeed it seemed renewed, revitalised. Ah, but then—as I came upon a second small knot of crewmen where they mumbled a few words over Stumpy Pete's wrapped corpse before launchin' it to a watery grave—I looked again at that glowin' thing, speculatin' at the *cost* of its newfound brilliance. . . .

"Then, turnin' from the rail, it happened I glanced in the direction of Black Jake and Zhadia's cabin situated under the afterdeck. The door was somewhat ajar and there she stood, half-hidden from view in the shadows of the cabin, gazin' out across the deck. Aye, and what was Zhadia's gaze rapt upon but the sky-cloth's golden glow, its shimmerin' warp and weave as it wafted so lazy like on the wind. Except . . . now the strangest thing of all, for I saw how the sky-cloth *ignored* the wind; it failed to fly leeward of the blow but instead seemed attracted to Zhadia; it wafted *diagonally* or *side-on*, appearin' to drift towards her! And I suddenly found myself thinkin' a crazy thought: how if it hadn't been made fast in the riggin' it might have attempted to fly right into Zhadia's eager arms!

"But just then Zhadia saw me lookin'; she retreated out of sight, reluctantly I thought, and closed the door. And as quick as you like with Zhadia's exit, the sky-cloth quit its hypnotic weavin' and fell into formless folds, for all its lustre like a lifeless rag hangin' there in the riggin'. . . ."

The atmosphere in the Hartlepool graveyard had grown heavy now, full of the oppressiveness of air that is usually the harbinger of bad weather. It might almost seem that the tropical storm of the dead pirate's tale had somehow conjured or evoked this one; but no, for Harry had anticipated its coming ever since leaving the old stone harbour in the antique town's most northerly quarter. And now that Billy Browen had chosen this moment to pause, perhaps to reassess, readjust his story's pace and progress, so the Necroscope found himself presented with the ideal opportunity to take stock of more mundane things—

—Which took him but a moment, until:

"Billy," he said, "I fear that if I remain here any longer I'm going to get wet. As it is I'm all cramped up, and if I die of pneumonia you'll never get the tale told, now will you?" And as if to illustrate his complaints he grunted, "*Uh!*" as he made the effort to rise and straighten up . . . which happened to coincide with the first of the heavy raindrops, one of which landed inside his collar. Then, as he stretched himself and flexed the muscles of his legs to ease the cramps:

Now, now, Harry! the ex-pirate chided. *Don't you know it's bad luck to talk of dyin'—not to mention in very bad taste—especially if you're talkin' to someone who's already dead?*

Nodding, Harry answered, "You know, you're probably right? But since speaking to the dead is my lot there's not much I can do about it. Anyway, it hasn't hurt me so far." *And heaven only knows I've done enough of it!* Which was a thought Harry kept to himself, though not for any reason that came easily to mind.

On the far side of the graveyard the caretaker was locking heavy iron gates. In the deepening gloom of a dreary, worsening evening he'd failed to observe that the usually neglected cemetery had a visitor. The Necroscope had noticed him, however, and now to maintain his advantage he turned up his collar and stepped back into the shade of the trees.

Then as the rain came on in earnest, he spoke again to the ex-pirate, this time in Billy Browen's own deadspeak mode. *It's time I was off, Billy. But I'll admit you've got me interested. So weather permitting I'll return some time tomorrow, or if not then as soon as possible. And that's a promise.*

Excellent! came the other's deadspeak sigh—once again of gratitude, or possibly inordinate relief?—*I'm already lookin' forward to it . . . er, Harry?*

But as the wind whipped the trees and the leaden raindrops

came squalling down, spattering like a myriad miniature eggs on the slabs and markers, the ex-pirate's words went unheard, lost to the deadspeak aether. For the Necroscope was no longer listening, indeed he was no longer there. . . .

Early the next morning, waking up alone in his lonely, rambling old house standing well off the beaten track near the hamlet of Bonnyrig, some miles from Edinburgh, Harry found himself with a headache; which was unusual for the Necroscope. It was also unusual that he was alone and "at home." For during this phase of his life a lot of his time—and in fact almost every night—was spent with Bonnie Jean Mirlu at her place in the city. B.J. was away right now, however, paying a visit to a relative or an old friend of the family whom Harry had heard her refer to only as "Auld John," in a place called Inverdruie "up north;" a fact which one of the girls B.J. employed as a hostess or barmaid in her Edinburgh wine bar had passed on to him by telephone only a minute or two after he had exited the Möbius Continuum into his living room on the previous evening.

Now, on reflection, and with B.J. in mind, the Necroscope reconsidered the frequency of his headaches and their possible cause or origin. For while just a moment ago he had misrepresented his current condition as "unusual"—which, for as long as he could remember, was exactly what such migraines had *used* to be—the truth of it was that since B.J.'s advent headaches and inexplicable periods of forgetfulness and absentmindedness had become not so much unusual as prevalent!

Suddenly realising that he was at cross-purposes with himself, Harry shrugged irritably. Oh, she was definitely one deep and mysterious lady, this Bonnie Jean! So perhaps his migraines came from trying to fathom the unfathomable, comprehend the unknowable and tame the completely untameable? For after all, who else but B. J. Mirlu would have the sheer gall, the impertinence to refer to the cold vampire killer and Necroscope, Harry Keogh, as her "wee man," and order him home like a little boy who had stayed out too late at night? Which, on several occasions, she had done! And these were orders with which Harry had willingly complied, at that!

Of course, B.J. wasn't aware of his . . . but his what? His secret identity, like Lois Lane with Clark Kent? She was privy to as little of Harry's metaphysical talents and previous life as he to hers; but he felt fairly sure that even if she suspected he was somehow different or special it wouldn't change anything very much, because he was *that* much under her spell—and she knew it! But still Harry fancied (however erroneously) that this "spell" he was under was no supernatural thing. No, it was her incredible sensuality that attracted him, or which—while he continued to deny the reality of it—more properly held him fast, besotted and in thrall; simply that rather than some dark and esoteric magic. And he smiled as he wondered:

Can too much sex give a man migraines?

On the other hand—as another sharp, stabbing pain struck him in his temple, banishing his smile and causing him to wince—on the *other* hand, it was ridiculous to even jokingly ascribe blame for this current headache to B. J. Mirlu when it was plain that its source was something else entirely. . . .

It had been there ever since he'd woken up—perhaps even before that—as part of a dream. Now, while toasting bread and making himself a pot of coffee, a frown creased the Necroscope's forehead as he attempted to bring that dream back into focus:

In it he had heard the murmur of several deadspeak voices whispering secretively amongst themselves, their owners apparently arguing about some shadowy thing—some danger, perhaps?—concerning himself. This, at least, was definitely not unusual; as well as fantasies conjured by the sleeping mind, people frequently dream scenarios and situations regarding the trials and tribulations of their waking lives, dreams that are often problem-solving mechanisms that discard the accumulated debris and mental garbage of mundane life and allow more serious problems—and sometimes, albeit rarely, their resolutions—to surface: in a word, oneiromancy. However, while Harry knew of Kekulé von Stradonitz's renowned "benzine ring" revelation, here the knowledge was redundant: he could rely on past, personal experience of the phenomenon.

Returning to the actual dream: the Necroscope could remember very little of it, and then only vaguely, as viewed through or muffled by a thick mist. In particular he recalled his frustration in trying to eavesdrop the deadspeak conversation. As to its source, however: he had somehow been left with the impression that the whispering voices had emanated from the Hartlepool cemetery. But there had been something else, indeed a *lot* more than that to it.

And there it was, the source of his headache: that buzzing or humming, the deadspeak static Harry had felt or sensed while talking to the ex-pirate, Billy Browen. And that really *was* unusual: that an hitherto unknown effect, first sensed in a deadspeak conversation, should later manifest itself in a dream so forcefully, insistently, that upon waking the Necroscope continued to experience its echoes or reverberations as a migraine. A man might dream of cancer but would be vastly unfortunate to wake up *with* a tumor! A person might dream he was on fire—but was most unlikely to spring awake charred and blistered! Well, not unless he really *was* on fire. . . .

As the Necroscope ate breakfast and the stabbing pains in his head gradually died away, he cast his mind back to the time he had spent—no more than an hour or two—in the incorporeal company of Billy Browen. It was shortly after the ex-pirate had begun to tell his story that Harry had first sensed this irregularity, this impression that the psychic aether's volume—or rather his sensitivity to such emissions from beyond—had somehow, suddenly been turned way up. At the time he had thought it might be simply another indication of his burgeoning parapsychological powers, but as Billy's story had progressed—

—So the intensity of the static had increased, apparently in parallel; and again, remembering his first impression of it, Harry likened it to the monotonous electrical hum of a record-player's speakers when the turntable is empty and the volume is turned up far too high. But in fact the turntable—or in this case the medium or instrumentality of the metaphysical aether—had *not* been empty; rather it had been the channel by which the Necroscope and Billy Browen communicated. Similarly, their deadspeak thought processes had been analogous to a spinning record.

And now Harry frowned again, thinking: *Why, by the time it started raining last night, our "private" conversation, or more properly Billy's story, would have been sounding out across the entire psychic spectrum! It may well have been "heard"* throughout *the dark domain, by all of the dead in their graves!*

But done with breakfasting and on checking this theory out with several dead friends in graveyards near and far, Harry discovered that he was quite wrong: not one of them had sensed any powerful or otherwise extraordinary emmissions in the deadspeak aether, and they assured the Necroscope that if *his* voice—and his warmth—had been broadcast in excessive volume, then they would surely have sensed, heard, and recognised him at once.

Which begged the questions: if the metaphysical volume had been deliberately turned up high, to what unknown realm and for what purpose had the Necroscope and Billy Browen's conversation been transmitted? And was it simply a deadspeak anomaly, or had there been someone there—wherever "there" was—to tune in on it?

A little while later, after thinking things through without arriving at any firm conclusion, but in a puzzled, far more cautious frame of mind, Harry returned via the Möbius Continuum to the ancient cemetery in Hartlepool. . . .

At ten in the morning the place was still very gloomy; the day was overcast, with patchy-grey, slow-moving clouds. Harry felt a depression of atmosphere—even of the psychic atmosphere— which caused him to shiver involuntarily, affecting him spiritually as well as physically.

As before, he had emerged from the Möbius Continuum behind the buttressed pier in the high stone wall, where he'd listened for a moment or two to the muffled thunder of traffic from outside, and to the cemetery's silence within, before stepping out to walk the weathered, weed-grown flags and gravel chippings of the principal pathway. Now, having crossed the venerable burial ground down that aisle of abandoned plots, lichened markers and occasional mausoleums—on the approach to the far, high perimeter wall where it stood in the shade of overhanging greenery— the Necroscope branched off from the central path and traversed the remaining distance at an angle which would deliver him more surely and directly to that lonely corner where the ex-pirate's grave lay beneath its unmarked, mottled marble slab.

And it was there—almost within sight of Billy Browen's plot— that the Necroscope slowed to a gradual, uncertain halt, frowning and fingering his chin, and glancing this way and that as if searching for some unknown, inimical thing . . . or perhaps in recognition of an uneasy premonition: the feeling that something here was somehow different, changed.

But what?

He stared at untended plots now shrouded in brambles, and at ancient, ivied markers which alone indicated the low, burial mounds of various long-forgotten persons . . . and wondered why a handful of these were not so much convex as concave, sunken in. Ground subsidence, he supposed, where the earth had been packed too loosely, too long ago; and then again, even the best timber of centuried coffins isn't going to last forever.

As for the tenants of these graves: surely by now they had moved on into better places, warmer climes? Or perhaps not; for after all, a certain dead Viking of Harry's recent acquaintance was still rolling around on the seabed. And so, on a whim, the Necroscope directed a deadspeak query into the earth, which was answered not at all. But at the same time he sensed a shrinking or reticence from certain more recent plots lying a little farther away whose occupants were still "in residence," as it were, and not yet ascended. They had obviously sensed his warmth, his presence, but the customary babble of excitement—and perhaps even a deadspeak greeting or two—were not forthcoming.

Come to think of it, there had been this same almost preternatural silence yesterday evening during the Necroscope and Billy Browen's initial conversation. Well of course anything to do with Harry's talents might be called "preternatural," but he applied the term from his personal viewpoint, scarcely aware of any paradoxical sophistry however inadvertent.

He might have further pondered, or even mentioned "aloud," the curious silence of the cemetery's departed, if Billy Browen had not chosen that precise moment to issue a timely deadspeak welcome:

Harry? Is it you? But of course it is! Certainly! Who else but the Necroscope announces his presence with the warm waft of a candle's flame? A small warmth to be sure, but a livin' spark for all that, and a most welcome one. And everythin' I've heard of you is true, for indeed you've kept your promise!

Without further pause Harry moved to the ex-pirate's plot, seating himself as before on Billy's blank marble marker. Then, answering the other's greeting with a less than amicable frown, he said, "My friend—if indeed you are my friend—it appears there's something not quite right here, but as yet I'm not sure what it is."

Ah! said Billy. *And you think perhaps that's my fault, eh? You'll be talkin' about the other inmates here, am I right? But surely you're aware, Harry, of how the decent dead shun criminality? I know you are. They'll have no truck with such as me—murderers and the like—and my wicked past of which I admitted the very first time we met. Didn't I speak of acts committed in the cut and thrust of things that I'm not proud of? It's one of the reasons I'm so glad I can speak to you, because the rest of 'em don't listen too well, or if they do don't answer.*

Well, and the ex-pirate could be right at that. And listening again to the graveyard's hush, the Necroscope thought: If I were to close my eyes, it would feel like I was in a dark room where unseen others were holding their breath, listening and waiting. But waiting for what? I feel that I'm on trial—that I'm being tested by the teeming dead—without knowing why. Is it that in befriending Billy Browen, however temporarily, I've broken some code or other? Have I really disappointed the Great Majority to such an extent?

He could of course ask but his pride wouldn't let him. And in any case there might well be another solution to the enigma, perhaps connected to that low, almost electrical hum of unknown energies which once again had commenced to permeate the metaphysical aether. Maybe the monotonous drone was creating an impenetrable screen to shut Harry and the ex-pirate off from the rest of the cemetery's incorporeal spirits? If this was the case and the screen had been erected *by* the graveyard's teeming dead . . . then indeed they'd taken against Billy Browen, and even the Necroscope's standing was in jeopardy. It would mean that while he had to do with Billy, they would have nothing to do with him.

Well, so be it. And stiffening, Harry refused to be deterred; he had made Billy a promise and he intended to keep it.

His thoughts in this respect had been deadspeak; there had been no need to hide them from the ex-pirate, whose weird story the Necroscope now intended to hear out to the end. And:

Bravo! said Billy. *I know you are their hero, for even the dead need their heroes, but I ask you, Harry: am I not one such lonely lich in my own right? Indeed I am. And alone in my grave I have but you to talk to. Very well, and now to the rest of my story . . .*

"Let me remind you," the ex-pirate recommenced his tale, "of my vows to olden shipmates—aye, even these centuries later, when all the names and the places, the deeds and damnations, are all but forgotten except to such as myself—that there are things I may not give name to for fear of the curses of those selfsame comrades: maledictions that may still be extant even though the men who uttered them are not. For if you'll grant me the ownership of my conscience, I suffer from curses enough without that I call down more!

"And so I repeat, there are places I may speak of without sup- plyin' their actual names or locations, which you may think you recognize even though I shall refuse to confirm such guesswork: far islands, whose soils might or might not be repositories for buried treasure; also the names I give to my principal characters, which once more as before may or may not be real.

"For example, that of young Will Moffat, who was happy to spend so much time up in the crow's-nest, him bein' so healthy, handsome and all, and havin' now and then found himself over a barrel, if you get my meanin'. For the rough-and-ready crew of the old *See Witch*—bein' so often under sail and deprived of their manly pleasures, as it were—well, they weren't especially particular.

"Ah, but it wasn't only certain perverted members of the crew who from time to time fancied young Will! And since there was only one passenger aboard . . . well, you'll know of course who I'm referrin' to. Black Jake's woman, Zhadia, that's who!

"Oh, I had seen her checkin' Will out behind Jake's back, lookin' the lad up and down, her eyes narrowin' when she stared at his firm-muscled arms, his thighs in worn canvas shorts when the weather was warm—and possibly when she was hot?—and his eyes blue as the tropical sea itself. What's more, I'd seen him lookin' back: just an occasional glance when Jake was otherwise engaged, but enough that it told a story all its own. . . .

"As for where we left off: there'd been this storm, you'll recall, which Black Jake Johnson had let the *Sea Witch* ride out to its very last blow. Now, havin' made a few small repairs, we were on course under slackenin' canvas for an island well known for its accep- tance of pirates and their booty. It may have been Cap'n Thomas Tew's colony at Libertilia, or maybe St. Mary's off Madagascar, or perhaps Port Royal in Jamaica across the rollin' South Atlantic: take your pick. That last mentioned, however—Jamaica, whose

Port Royal was accredited with bein' the richest wickedest city in the New World, and not without good reason—might make an excellent choice . . . on which subject I shall say no more.

"Anyway, what should happen but with land clear visible on the horizon to the west, the breeze fell away and again we were becalmed. That close to port, no more than three or four miles, Cap'n Jake could have ordered the oars manned; but night comin' down and the danger with shallows, reefs, and what have you, instead we dropped anchor and broke open a keg of rum. We'd had a good run and the hold was full of filched treasures—not least silver, spices, and gold ingots—and once the crew got theirs . . . well, the last thing Black Jake wanted was that they should jump ship out of spite or perhaps because of perceived meanness on his part, to live off their loot in luxury in some mountain-clingin' town or jungle plantation, and leavin' us short-handed. And anyway if the old *Sea Witch*'s canvas was hangin' slack then so was everyone else's, and no one, neither friend nor foe, was goin' to come up on us unexpected like. Also, with a good drunk and a decent night's kip behind them, the crew would be fightin' fit when finally they went ashore to whatever awaited them, not knackered out from haulin' on the long oars.

"And so it was we had a rip-roarin' singsong and shindig, drinkin' our fill and sleepin' it off wherever we should chance to fall; all but the night watch, that is, one Long Tom Fellows—so called because tip to toe he was a fathom and then some—who would only drink water or, when it was in short supply, his own sweet piss! Oh yes, and one other noticeable absentee from much of the merriment: young Will Moffat, that clean-limbed lad who knew when it was as well to keep out of the way.

"Ah, but by now you're surely thinkin': all very well, but what of the sky-cloth? Rightly so, for that's what this tale is all about. . . .

"Well, that glittery stuff was still there in the riggin'. Why? Partly because Jake had ordered it left there, 'to stiffen up a bit,' whatever that meant, but also because the lads who'd salvaged it had suffered these peculiar blisters on their hands like jellyfish stings . . . which probably were just such stings, for the sea had been full of these Portuguese man-o'-war things that time. Not that the sky-cloth had lost its allure: not by a long shot. Even durin' their drinkin' and jiggin', this or that member of the crew would stagger over to where it dangled lifeless, just within reach, and you could see their eyes beginnin' to glaze over—them that weren't already glazed—from lookin' at it, and you just knew that the urge was there in all of them to reach up and touch it. Aye, even with its golden glow fadin' to bronze as the light failed, still it exercised a weird fascination. . . .

"Come mornin', I woke up on the naked deck with a throbbin' in my head that made every creak of the *Sea Witch*'s timbers a cannon shot, and Black Jake's boot in my ribs soberin' me up quick as you like. 'Up, ye drunken swab,' says he (uncommonly subdued language in view of the prevailin' circumstances). 'Up on yer feet, Mister, for we've a fuckin' problem!' Which was more like it.

" 'Long Tom Fellows is staggerin' about with a lump like a hen laid an egg on his head!' the Cap'n went on as I scrambled. 'It appears he's been out of things most of the night! The sky-cloth has disappeared, and so have Zhadia and fuckin' Will Moffat! They took the rowboat, curse 'em to every hell, but I can't say for a fact if Will stole Zhadia or she stole him! Whichever it be, young Moffat has bought himself a one-way ticket to Davy Jones' domain, and Zhadia's black eyes will be a sight blacker when I catches up with that treacherous slut!'

"So Jake averred, and I never knew him to break a vow. Not one such as this: the result of a most personal affront—which is to say the very least, I'm sure you'll agree.

"Ah, but how to catch up with them, who'd had all night to row ashore? And it wasn't as if Will and the woman couldn't pay their way, for the lad had taken his share—and possibly a bit more—from the stash where an excess of booty had been lodged like ballast in the hold, when the Cap'n couldn't fit it all in his cabin. Which wasn't the end of Jake's run of evil luck, for the sea stayed flat as a Dover sole's white belly for a further nine hours or so, and we didn't arrive in port until the afternoon. And no sign of Will and Zhadia, or even the rowboat which would be hidden away somewhere under ocean-fringin' greenery.

"Well, for the next fortnight Black Jake sailed around and stomped about that tropical island—which I promise you was no mere atoll with just three or four coconut palms, but well over a thousand, maybe closer to *two* thousand square miles of mountains, plains, and skeeter-ridden rivers and jungle—askin' his questions, offerin' rewards, searchin' high and low for the runaways, and flarin' into murderous rages each time he was disappointed. Until in a while certain members of the crew gave up on him and one by one began to disperse into the island's various, mainly nefarious communities.

"Which absenteeism, when I brought it to Jake's attention, did the trick and caused him to see sense. For there was treasure out at sea and a man must make his fortune while he's able, else live out his life and die in poverty. And as for women . . . well Jake could always find himself another black-eyed girl, if not another Zhadia. . . .

"And so we replaced the half-dozen men who'd sneaked away, hirin' four and shanghaiin' two more, then put back out to sea proper; followin' which for a six-month we discovered the true nature of hard work. Not that piratin' was ever soft work, but by reason of his loss, his damaged pride, Cap'n Jake was grown more crabby, more ill-tempered, and downright brutal than ever. And for almost two hundred days we suffered his tongue-lashin', his *real* lashin's, and general bullyin', until one and all we'd had more than a sufficiency.

"Why, it got so bad I could sense mutiny brewin' and might even have led it myself; but then at last, from the lone survivor of a vessel we'd taken after one hell of a battle—taken, then sent to the bottom—Cap'n Jake heard a story that at once changed his nature and cheered him up no end. It was this:

"That on the selfsame outlaw island where we reckoned Will Moffat and Zhadia were hidin' out, somethin' was goin' on which had gone on before but never with such enterprise. In a little-known jungle bolt-hole, a ramshackle place of no previous importance, treasure in the shape of jewels, doubloons, silver ingots, and pieces of eight were changin' hands quick as cards could be dealt and dice rolled; rum was bein' swilled like so much water, and high-priced women of all colours were available by the hour to whoever could afford 'em. Which mightn't seem so extraordinary—at least, not on *that* island—if not for the fact that the description of the proprietors of this den of ill or iller repute, not to mention those of a certain large handful of its frequenters, rang bells galore!

"Aye, for it seemed more than likely that the latter were the *Sea Witch*'s half-dozen deserters, now gamblin', whorin, or otherwise throwin' away their by no means paltry take from Jake Johnson's share-out after our last venture; for however mean he was in his captainin', it would be an untruth to say Cap'n Jake was mean with the booty he could never have amassed without the brute force of his pirate crew. For which reason the Cap'n kept but two shares of a prize while his officers, includin' myself, got one and a half, and each of the men got one. Ah, but divide fifty into *fifty thousand* . . . and it's one hell of a share! Or, in this case, six shares.

"So then, the rise of this new seat of iniquity might well be explained by the big pay-outs to our half-dozen ship-jumpers, while naturally any rumoured superabundance of loot, liquor, and ladies of pleasure would have attracted well-heeled pirate scum from all quarters, until the den was its current centre of sinful activity. But the clincher where Cap'n Jake was concerned—the fact that guaranteed our return to the island in question—was as stated the description of the proprietors of this jungle hideaway. And I'll wager you've already guessed it:

"That the one was a brawny lad in silk shirt and pants, a mere youth with a golden ring in one ear, a brace of pistols in his belt, wearin' a chain of doubloons as a necklace, and rings of gold on each finger of his shrivelled hands . . . which looked like they'd been scarred by acid or burned in a fire. And Cap'n Jake remembered how Will Moffat had used to wear a gold ring in his ear; also, how the men who brought the sky-cloth aboard had been burned as by jellyfish stings. And then there was this:

"The description of a *female* proprietor who kept mainly to herself but would come out from time to time on a balcony overlookin' the main gamin' room, to stare down on all the gamblin' and drinkin' and revelry; a young woman with long, agile hands, long legs, the slender shape of a goddess, and eyes dark as the night. A rare beauty, aye—a seeming treasure in her own right—whose only fault would seem to be that she never smiled, and whose only dress was a scintillant golden wrap that she wore on one shoulder and down round her chest and hips in a spiral like them Indian women sometimes dress. And that dress, while it appeared to sit on her light as a feather, gleamed so like gold it was easily mistaken for the precious metal itself. And both the dress and the woman, they were so dazzlin' to the eyes of every man who saw them that the balcony was guarded at the stairs and both ends by fat men out of Arabia, eunuchs who would use their scimitars to cut a man down as soon as look at him, if ever the woman's allure tempted any such fool to try and attend her.

"It had to be Cap'n Jake's Zhadia, of course—or rather, Will Moffat's Zhadia—for who else could she possibly be? And as for her golden dress . . .

"Well, need I say more?"

That last was a question which, because Harry was vaguely aware that it required an answer, woke him up. Straightening up, from where he now found himself slumped to the right on the low flat perch of Billy's marker, he shuddered and started, blinking his eyes and wondering what was happening here. In fact, just for a moment before he achieved *almost* full awareness, Harry couldn't even have said where he was or what he was doing!

And as for that confounded *droning*—why, it could drive a man mad! Maybe it *was* driving him mad! But then:

Eh? What? said Billy, trying but failing to sound entirely surprised. *Are you still with me, Necroscope? Or is my story so borin' you were about to fall asleep on me?*

Falling asleep on Billy? Had he been? Well if so he hadn't realised it, and felt fairly sure that he'd taken in every word of the ex-pirate's story so far! He *had* heard Billy's question, hadn't he? About Zhadia, and Billy not needing to say any more? Yes, certainly he had—and yet it was still as if he'd been in some kind of trance, like an iron filing trapped in the grip of a magnetic field . . . what, galvanised? Or maybe hypnotised? And even now he felt that his metaphysical mind was gyrating just a little outside its accustomed orbit, as if he'd had too much to drink; and he couldn't be sure that the rest of him was working correctly either! And so:

"What?" said the Necroscope, as much to himself as to anyone else, still bewildered by his circumstances. And "*Ouch!*" as he straightened up and went to clasp his throbbing head . . . only to find his right hand clogged with damp soil where he'd pulled his fist from the grave dirt! That was why he had been toppling to the right: because for some utterly inexplicable reason he'd been thrusting his fingers deep into the earth, still damp from yesterday's rain.

Ouch? Billy had meanwhile repeated him, still somewhat unconvincingly concerned. *Are you hurt?*

"Hurting? Yes I am!" said the Necroscope, nodding however carefully. "It's my head . . . I think it's coming apart from all this buzzing! What on earth . . . I mean what the *hell* is it, and why does it keep getting louder?"

Buzzin'? Billy repeated him, apparently puzzled. *You mean that far-off dronin' like the thrummin' of taut riggin'? Yes, I hear it, too, though not so much that it bothers me. But surely it's an effect of your powerful talents? So I assumed, anyway.*

"What's that you say? Far-off?" Harry was astonished. "You mean it sounds distant to you? Well not to me, Billy! More like it's right on top of me!"

He sensed the other's deadspeak shrug—no, he even *felt* it, because of the increased volume of whatever it was that had to be shaking not only him but surely the entire psychic aether—and in the next moment reeled from the abrupt, totally unexpected change as suddenly the dull hammer blows stopped falling on his temples . . . stopped instantly, cut off at the source, where- or whatever that was! And:

So maybe it was you causin' it after all! said the ex-pirate. *For now it's gone, stopped almost as soon as you mentioned it. I mean no offence, Necroscope, but it seems to me that it's all of your own doin', all in that powerful mind of yours.*

It could well be at that! Indeed, Harry felt that even if he or Billy Browen had been "whispering" during that last deadspeak session, still it would have sounded like they were bellowing! But on the other hand he'd also begun to associate these monotonous migraine-generating reverberations with proximity to Billy himself. And so, since the latter seemed to have reached a natural break in his weird narrative, the Necroscope decided that he, too, would take a break . . . from the now enigmatic Mr. Browen. Not that he wouldn't be back, for whatever had gone on/was going on here, Harry now made a vow with himself to see it through, tracking it down to the last.

For which reason:

"Billy—" he said, wincing and screwing up his eyes, half-expecting the echoes of that single word to sound like so much thunder in his head, and sighing his relief when it didn't, "I think maybe we should break off for an hour or so." And with a glance at his wristwatch he went on: "It will soon be my lunch hour. I know a place where I can eat something and wash it down with half a beer and a couple of aspirins. So I'm afraid you'll have to excuse me now."

And before the other could reply or query the Necroscope's intentions, Harry got unsteadily to his feet, stepped forward a pace, then one more, or at least half a one—

—And was no longer there . . .

The small cafe only a few streets inland from Old Hartlepool's harbour in that most hoary part of town, a place the Necroscope and his then girlfriend Brenda had visited from time to time on their long lovers' walks, perhaps to eat a sandwich and drink a cup of vile coffee, was still there. Fortunately, a dilapidated chemist's store stood just two shopfronts away, and there Harry bought a strip of aspirins before entering the cafe and seating himself at a small, grubby table.

Along with a cup of coffee, just as vile as he remembered, and a half-decent bacon sandwich, he took three of the tablets, and was pleased to note that his headache was fast receding. It was possible, however, that this was because Harry had shielded himself from the psychic aether by "switching off," as it were, his macabre skills; which concerned him more than a little: the thought that the droning might now be a regular condition, immanent to his use of metaphysics.

This was something that Harry could put to the test immediately, and done with eating he did just that: opening his mind however tentatively to tune in on what he hoped would be familiar background emanations from a place beyond life. And for all that he was prepared to back off in a moment and let his unique mind snap shut, indeed those murmurings from the psychic aether were familiar and mostly free of the droning anomaly. Listening intently, Harry thought it possible he detected a far faltering thrumming . . . which quickly faded and soon died away entirely.

And now in its place—finding a path through the ethereal babble and background chatter—came something else: a "voice," no longer quite so bold or boastful as before, which the Necroscope nevertheless recognised at once.

Harry? said the voice of that recent, now somewhat subdued acquaintance. *Harry, if that's you, and I'm sure it is, I think you should know you have a problem.*

"Erik Haroldson?" said the Necroscope, getting to his feet and preparing to leave the cafe. "You're one persistent drowned Viking, I'll grant you that! So what's up now?"

The fat proprietor, looming close where he collected empty cups and plates, paused and cocked his head on one side. "I beg your pardon?" he said. "Something else I can do for you?"

"Er, no," Harry replied, as he mentally kicked himself. It wasn't like him to make that kind of mistake, but right now his concentration appeared to be wandering. And erecting his mental shields, securing his mind, he explained: "No, I was just sort of talking to myself, that's all." And grinning apologetically, he shrugged it off as best possible.

"Hmm!" The other nodded and got on with his work, commenting: "Myself, I do it all the time. So we'd best watch it, you and me! They do say it's the first sign!"

Leaving the cafe, Harry cut through narrow alleys between mainly neglected streets and walked to the harbour. It had been his intention to go straight back to the graveyard—he'd felt somehow *drawn* back there, and even anxious to return—but Erik Scarhelm Haroldson seemed to be offering him some kind of warning . . . or was that merely an inducement, bait to trap him into another fruitless conversation? Well, he would soon find out.

Arriving at the antique harbour's weathered wall, the Necroscope finally relaxed his shields and used deadspeak to renew his contact with the long-dead reaver. However, since there was no other living soul within earshot or even in sight, he voiced his thoughts out loud, which had always seemed the simplest way to do it. "Did you mention a problem, Erik? What, with a garrulous 'Varyargi' bully, perhaps?"

Climbing up onto the broad wall and seating himself in the

same spot he'd occupied yesterday, he looked out across ruffled water and waited for Erik's response. Instead of which . . . what was that sudden, furious background babble all about?

And that's the problem! declared Erik, barely able to make himself heard above the deadspeak interference. *The Great Majority, as they're wont to call themselves, or the teeming dead as they actually are. But tell me: can it be true that you haven't noticed anything, well,* odd *about their behaviour, Necroscope?*

Harry narrowed his eyes and mind both. Now that the Viking came to mention it, he had indeed noticed just such peculiarities: a certain reticence in those he'd spoken to other than the ex-pirate; an aura of hushed expectancy from the dead lodged in the old cemetery, and also from them an unaccustomed evasion of contact, creating a generally uneasy silence in the parapsychological aether where Harry's living warmth had always been most welcome.

It was simply—or maybe not so simply—this: that while for the time being the Great Majority didn't expressly shun the Necroscope, neither did they particularly desire to acknowledge or accommodate his presence.

And there you have it, said Erik, who was privy to Harry's powerful thoughts even over the anonymous deadspeak flak.

"And that's it?" said Harry. "You believe I have a problem because sometimes even the dead appreciate a little privacy and prefer to keep themselves to themselves?" Which was sheer sophistry and fooled no one.

Hah! It's a lot more than that and you know it! the Viking declared. *And anyway I haven't told you anything yet. And also, it's hard to say why I should want to! You're a very ungrateful man, Necroscope, and I'm tempted to keep what I know to myself!*

"Then why don't you?" Harry snapped, and at once relented. It wasn't his way: to deal harshly or cruelly with the dead. Oh he believed in an eye for an eye, but Erik had done him no real harm and it now seemed that the Viking actually wanted to protect or at least to warn him of some perceived danger.

For which reason: "Look, I'm sorry," said the Necroscope abruptly. "We got off to a bad start yesterday; I was feeling a bit low. As for you . . . well, let's face it: deep-sunken as you are, you're *always* a bit low! Er, that is to say your bones . . . I mean you, physically, or what's left of you!" But then, realising how inept his words must sound, Harry bit his tongue.

The thick-skinned Viking, however, hadn't noticed—or in any case chose to ignore—Harry's gaffe, and said: *Well then, perhaps we can be friends after all? Or if not friends, acquaintances at least?*

"Of course, gladly!" said Harry relievedly. "So then, what else did you want to tell me? But quickly, Erik, if you please, for I've things to do, somewhere I must go."

You're eager to be off, then? (Which was said in a certainly, calculating undertone.)

At which that psychic babble once more rose up like a wall of sound, purposely contrived to block Harry and the Viking's conversation. Astonished and angry, still the Necroscope remembered to switch to his "silent" deadspeak mode—before shouting into the psychic aether and demanding to know:

Now what the hell is all this? Exclude me if you wish, for whatever reason, and this Viking too, but don't you go interfering in my business! If I've done something you don't agree with, tell me about it by all means—that's if or when you decide to talk to me again—but until then get off my back AND SHUT THE HELL UP!

Almost at once the clamour died down, and Erik Haroldson's incorporeal voice was full of awe when he said: *Now that's more like it! Why, even my grumbling, grousing crew have fallen silent now!*

The Necroscope calmed down, and reverting to common speech he said, "Now perhaps you'll tell me what's going on?"

I can only tell you what I myself have been told, said the other. *And that was a long time ago.* Then, after a short pause: *Do you know—are you aware, Harry—what a hard lot the people of this coast really are? Well they are, and they have been forever and a day: long before my time and ever since.*

Harry sighed impatiently; he really couldn't see this getting him anywhere; now that the thrumming had stopped he wanted to hear the end of the ex-pirate's story, and already he'd been away from the old graveyard for quite some time. But finally he answered the Viking, saying: "I lived here, schooled here, came up with hard kids here. I know exactly how strong the people of this region are, and that they're the salt of the earth—which includes those of them who are down *in* the earth! And incidentally, anyone who knows me will tell you I'm not so soft myself. But what of it? What's this all about?"

In my time, said Erik, *these were especially hard people—but then they were hard times. I know I've told how cowards ran from us; well sometimes they did, but not always. That time when they sank us in the harbour, they had been waiting for us; they wanted to make us pay for other raids we'd carried out; for our thieving, our burning, and our attacks on their women. And they did. Looking back, I suppose we deserved it. We were in our way pirates no less than your more recent varieties, except we were among the earliest of the breed; indeed the "Varyargi" were all of seven centuries earlier than the one that you've been spending time with! Yet just as we were dealt with by this country's brave defenders— aye, even if they were common fisherman—so these more modern reavers were also dealt with . . . including, I fancy, the one in that old graveyard who relates his story from the earth beneath his marble* bautastein—*which is to say his marker. Aye, and it's possible I know a thing or two about that marble slab, too.*

The Necroscope's gradually failing interest at once sprang back to life. "What? You mean Billy Browen? Billy and his blank marker?"

Was that his name? The teeming dead erected such a barrier I could only make out snatches of your conversation. But still, if I remember correctly these many years later, that was indeed his name as last I heard it mentioned.

Intensely curious now, Harry enquired: "When was that, and in what connection was it mentioned?"

In yet another story, Necroscope: a tale I heard from one of Billy's shipmates—a younger man called Will Moffat—who was hanged from a gibbet next to Billy, right here on this wide harbour wall. That was . . . oh, a long time ago, even as much as three hundred years but certainly not far short!

"Tried as pirates, found guilty and hung for their crimes: Will and Billy both." Harry slowly nodded. "It explains Billy's unmarked plot in the old cemetery . . . at least he was buried in hallowed ground! But on the other hand, where's Will?"

Rotted all away on his gibbet, said Erik. *Which some said was a crime in itself, not simply because of his youth but also by reason of him not being right in the head. He'd taken such a clout to his skull that it shook his brain and left a scar that might even have rivalled my own! But where I had kept my senses Will's were robbed away. In death he got 'em back, and that was when I got to hear his story. The two of us being cut from much the same cloth, as it were, we could at least commune with each other if not with anyone else. But you'd un-derstand far better, Necroscope, if you'd let me tell it as I heard it.*

Another story? Harry was torn two ways; the ancient grave-yard called out to him and he wondered if he had time for this. And yet some instinct informed him that what the Viking knew of Will Moffat's story could be of great importance; that it might even be the key to all that was weird and mysterious here. But:

"Why can't Will tell his own story?" he enquired.

Because Will's no longer here, said the Viking. *Because he moved on many years ago. Something of a measure of the way he'd lived his life, I sup-pose. Shanghaied as little more than a pup, he had been forcefully apprenticed, as it were. Oh, he'd become a pirate in the end, because that was all he'd known! But someone somewhere has seen reason to forgive him, and now he's gone from here. Maybe one day me and mine will likewise be gone from here. Surely there are places in Valhalla even for Vikings such as us? At any rate we hope so.*

What, signs of conscience? In a blunt and boastful Viking? Pleasantly surprised, Harry nodded his approval. "I'm sure that you'll get there eventually," he said. "But before then I think maybe I should hear Will's story."

I shall gladly repeat it, said Erik. *But first . . . listen!* As he paused abruptly, dramatically, Harry could almost picture him cocking his head on one side in an attitude of intense concentration. Un-til: *Now tell me,* Erik finally continued, *what do you make of that?*

Harry listened, frowned, then answered sourly, "That's the Great

Majority. I don't know what they're up to—it's all very strange to me—but it seems they're throwing up another deadspeak wall."

Indeed they are! the Viking replied. *But that wall they're erecting now, it isn't between you and me, Necroscope. No, it's between us and a certain ancient graveyard! Now why is that, do you suppose?*

In answer to which, for the moment, Harry was silent—

—Until in a little while, changing the subject:

"I may already know some of Will's story," he said, as the Viking made ready to begin. "If it is the same story, then it's likely I've heard it to the point where Will and a woman called Zhadia set up a sort of, well, a refuge you might call it, on a jungled island where pirates of all kinds could feel reasonably safe from the justice of their various authorities. I also know that Captain Jake Johnson—called 'Black' Jake—was intent on finding, wreaking vengeance on Will, and taking back Zhadia, who the youth had stolen away from him. Oh, and the story also contains something about a shawl or cloak of shimmering golden sky-stuff."

So then! said the incorporeal reaver. *It is most certainly the same story! And this is how it continues:*

"Will Moffat knew that sooner or later Black Jake Johnson would hear of his tropical island venture, his den of various iniquities, and come looking for him, just as he'd looked before when Will and Zhadia were hiding in the jungle; for which reason the wily youth kept lookouts among the local peoples in the coastal towns, harbours, and even remote bays where the crews of vessels were wont to come ashore openly, or sometimes covertly, depending on their status or situation. These lookouts that Will used were paid in coins, rum, and promises: just enough to help them maintain an interest in his well-being.

"So that even as Jake careened the *Sea Witch* in just such a remote bay, there torturing one or two locals for their knowledge, Will learned that his ex-master, this brutal pirate, was coming for him. And he made what preparations he could, because he knew that this time Black Jake must surely find him. In fact Will was resigned to the fact that however long Jake took about it, the brute *would* eventually find him; it wasn't in the man's nature to leave unanswered such a slight as he had suffered.

"And with his ship stripped, careened on her side, and the bulk of his crew at work scraping and patching her bottom, Jake disguised himself as best possible, and along with Billy Browen and two other worthies took up what weapons he could manage and set off into the jungle to pay Will Moffat a visit.

"Meanwhile Will and Zhadia had prospered; or rather, truth to tell, in certain *ways* they had prospered—in their finances most definitely, in other ways not at all: more of which later, as the story unfolds—until their sanctuary at the base of a jungled hill had grown from a ramshackle, mosquito-ridden bolt-hole to a township of many leaning shacks with a central building which in its time must have been a veritable mansion. As big and bigger than the largest Viking meeting hall that I ever got drunk in, it was constructed on two levels that backed into the steep hillside, and the entire upper floor belonged to Will and Zhadia.

"Now, I've spoken of young Will's preparations, which were basic at best. He had informed certain of his patrons—half-a-dozen men, once members of the crew of the *Sea Witch*—of Black Jake's imminent arrival, and he'd placed a bounty on that one's head. Each man of the six had a 'pistol,' unheard-of weapons in Viking times, which fired small metal balls at such speeds that they would enter a man's heart and kill him! And of course they had knives and swords. And Will himself was likewise equipped.

"All very well, but what Black Jake had in addition to *his* weapons was a reputation for ferocity, cruelty, and most of all an astonishing longevity! For he'd committed piracy across what young Will was wont to call 'the seven seas,' oceans unknown in Viking times. He'd fought battles galore, not only with law officers and military men on land and sea, but with other hardened pirates too. He'd ground down as many crews as rotten teeth and *still* come through it all unscathed! Which was why the hard men who went with him to Will's and Zhadia's refuge were mainly unafraid of what might await them; the boldness, outrageous luck, and fighting skill of their chief—to say nothing of their own prowess in a battle—was sure to protect and keep them safe.

"As for 'Mister' Billy Browen: well it's possible he might have had his own agenda—not that events would work out in his favour, not ultimately—but that is to jump too far ahead, and this is a tale that should be allowed to unfold in its own good time. . . .

"So then, with the rains coming on, Jake and his men trekked the jungled interior, and because Will's lookouts sheltered from the weather they failed to intercept the *Sea Witch*'s captain and comrades-in-arms until that quartet was at the steps to the central structure's entrance. Which was when Jake came face-to-face with two of the six who had jumped ship on him—one of whom paid for his desertion with a single sword thrust, and the other with a razor-sharp blade across his windpipe.

'Then out of the rain and into the gaming area, which was bordered by bar rooms and the curtained alcoves of common prostitutes, stepped Black Jake and his men. Disguised and dripping wet, dispersing within the great smoky room, they moved quickly among the gamblers, whores, and rum-soaked revelers, where three more ex-members of the *Sea Witch*'s company were soon discovered and dealt with as quietly as possible. Until the sole surviving deserter—realizing what was happening: that ex-comrades, now murderous foemen, had infiltrated the jungled den and commenced a killing spree—raised a belated alarm before fleeing for his life.

"By then, with their presence only just discovered, Black Jake's avengers had come together again at the foot of sweeping stairs that climbed to a high, bead-curtained balcony overlooking in its entirety the hall of thronging gamers and roisterers. There on the stairs Jake's raiders were confronted by a pair of fat eunuchs wielding curving, broad-bladed swords, which proved of no use at all against point-blank pirate pistols; and in any case the time for stealth was now well past.

"Shot dead, the Arabs were felled; their blood flowed down the stairs while Jake and his party threw themselves up and on. And there at the sweep of the balcony they were met by two more eunuchs who they engaged with shot, swords, and knives.

"Meanwhile a majority of the drunken revellers in the great hall had woken up to the invasion, and because Jake and his men had disposed of their disguises, the roaring pirate Captain and his party had at last been recognized for the terrible men that they really were. Now down below—as cards and dice were scattered, tables overturned, and good rum spilled—a crush of both sober and sodden men, and shrieking whores alike, all surged in a panic for the crowded defile of the exit.

"But the pistol shots and screams—the uproar in general— had finally alerted others in the upstairs rooms, and now on the balcony stood a figure wrapped in a remarkable golden robe: Zhadia, of course, whose face was beautiful as always while yet seeming strangely vacant. And appearing alongside her, who else but young Will Moffat, who despite his rich raiment seemed likewise listless and withdrawn—and perhaps even resigned?—with eyes deep sunken in a sallow face.

"For a moment—one moment only—the tableau was frozen . . . then with his shortsword held high, with his dark eyes blazing and crooked teeth grinding, Black Jake rushed upon the pair. Young Will managed to put himself between his former master and Zhadia, the while fumbling a pistol from his silken sash—only to have it tumble from his palsied hand! Incredible, when with a twitch of just one finger he could have shot Black Jake Johnson stone dead! Ah, but Will's hands weren't what they used to be!

"Then Jake was upon him: with a 'Hah!' he raised his sword higher, and with a 'Ho!' brought it down on Will's head. It cut him deep, flattening him to the floor with a great bloody gouge in his skull. And now Jake straddled him, and up went his shortsword one more time. At which—

"—The strangest thing! For that was when 'Mister' Billy Browen shouldered Black Jake aside away from the more than half-stunned youth, and met his downward-hurtling blade with that of his own weapon, which causing sparks to fly and Jake to curse! And before the astonished Captain could explode in fury:

"'Now hold!' cried Billy, backing off beyond the immediate reach of his gape-mouthed master's wrath. And: 'Cap'n darlin',' he continued, 'Will's no more than a lad! Don't go killin' him, Jake! For there's nothin' to be gained—no fame or glory in it for you—naught but shame if it get out that you killed a mere whelp, and for nothin' more than to spite a treacherous woman!'

"All of this from young Will Moffat's mouth, you'll understand, just as he repeated it to me while he hung there rotting on a gibbet's arm; he having been aware of Billy's pleas on his behalf, where he'd writhed on the floor in a bloody daze.

"Now through all of this Zhadia had stood there, pale as a beautiful ghost, looking this way and that but blankly, with no expression whatsoever; she had to be in shock: which Black Jake and his men must surely have believed was the case. And now the cuckold—the cheated Captain—turned his rage upon her.

"He went to cut her down, barely in time checked the blow, and very nearly choked on the word as he called her a whore! He snatched at a loose corner of her golden gown where it lay flat to her shoulder, snarling: "All covered in gold, are we? And is yer body so very precious when a mere boy can have it for his pleasure whenever he fancies it, eh? And what of all those rum-soaked swabs down below? . . . How many of them have seen what's under that glitterin' rag? *Ye treacherous whore!*

"With which he yanked on the sky-stuff to rip it from her. But instead of tearing it simply *unwound* from Zhadia, as of its own accord; which with the force of Jake's tugging set her spinning, then staggering and toppling, as naked as a newborn child but by no means as pure, as the shimmering robe floated free of her. Naked she was, aye, poor creature . . . a poor lost soul, *in a body that was no longer beautiful but hideously transformed!*

"Moving in and out of consciousness, Will saw her and re-alised that what he'd been imagining ever since Zhadia first wore the golden thing—or ever since it first wore her!—was now real-ity. Black Jake saw it, too; he snatched back his hand in a frenzied attempt to break free of the weird mesh that was burning him like slow fire! He went to slash at it, cut it with his sword's sharp blade, but it wouldn't cut! And now as he cursed, stumbled, stamped, and hauled on his trapped hand, so the languidly waft-ing sky-stuff suddenly quickened and became imbued of a terrible purpose! In another moment it had wrapped Black Jake as in the scaly coils of some weird sea serpent!

"As Jake staggered to and fro with his black eyes starting out, down from within the golden sheath which now enveloped him fell the smoking ruins of his customary garments: scraps of his leather jacket, sailcloth trousers, melting silk shirt and sash. Also his weapons: all tumbling free from where he'd lodged them about his person, all black and smouldering as if painted with hot tar!

"He tottered there, obviously in agony, but such was Black Jake's enormous strength that he refused to go down! And all he said was this, which young Will heard clearly enough, before he passed out from his wound:

"'Look after me, Mister—and look after this young *bastard*, too—' With a kick in the ribs for Will. 'Aye, for I'm not yet done with this one. Ooh! *Argh!*' With which Jake's eyes sort of glazed over, and his mouth went slack; the pain was gone but so was his mind, most of it. And that was all young Will Moffat knew of things for a while, except that before he passed out he looked again at Zhadia where she'd fallen to the floor, and saw what he'd been caring for ever since the first time she dressed herself in the sky-stuff:

"From her neck up she was the same as ever, likewise from her knees down; but the shape she'd shown when swathed in gold, that had been a disguise, as false—or as normal?—in appearance as that sky-stuff had wanted her to look! For now she was a hag! No more the ravishing Zhadia, not in that ravished body, but an old, old woman: indeed a hag! Her breasts like withered, tattered sacks lying flat on her ribs, several of which showed ivory white and yellow where the sere skin had shrunk back from them. Her belly: blotched, blackened, and wrinkled; shriveled to leather like a dead thing laid out in the sun too long. And Zhadia's once-seductive, once-supple thighs and softly curving rump: now no more than skin over bone—and lacking even skin in more places than one!

"Young Will Moffat saw her like that, aye, and knew that his worst fears for her were realised. For in all those months since she first donned that robe—or thing, whatever it was—he had never been able to touch her. Oh, he'd tried, which accounted for the ruined claws he now wore for hands! And he also knew it for an act of mercy when Billy Browen cried his horror and loathing, then did for Zhadia what his Captain should have done, taking her head with his cleanly shining sword . . . !"

The Necroscope felt torn two ways. Now that Erik Haroldson had lost much of his bluster his manner of expression and dead-speak phrasing had acquired a genuine eloquence; there was no denying that he knew how to tell a tale. Nor could there be too much of Erik's—or young Will Moffat's, or Billy Browen's—story left to tell . . . and yet Harry felt a powerful compulsion, an urgent need, to return to the old graveyard and the last-mentioned ex-pirate.

These were the Necroscope's thoughts during the short interval while Erik paused and considered the best way to continue his narrative: unshielded thoughts that issued into the psychic aether as deadspeak, of course; to which, in such close proximity, the incorporeal Viking was privy. And something in what he had heard at once goaded him to a sharp enquiry:

What? Is it really so, Necroscope?

The tiny harbour's promenade and sea wall in the immediate vicinity were deserted, prompting Harry to use common speech as he gave himself a shake and replied: "Eh? Is what so?"

Why, that you're feeling a strange compulsion to return to that old grave-yard! If so, I beg you not to be in such a hurry. I fear there's danger in it, which the rest of this story might in part explain.

Harry gave an impatient sigh, shuffled about to adjust his position on the cold stone wall, and finally said, "Very well—but I'm pretty sure Billy Browen will think it unfair of us. He commenced this story, after all; you've continued it . . . surely he should be the one to finish it! Don't you think so?"

What I think, the Viking answered, *is that you should hear the rest of it from me. Or at least enough that you can make up your own mind.*

And now it was Harry's turn to query: "But make up my mind about what?"

Ah, if only I knew for sure! the other answered, in such a way that the Necroscope could sense the frustrated shake of his head.

Then, before Harry could change his mind, the Viking continued the story. . . .

"Billy Browen's party was now reduced to himself and two others from the *Sea Witch*'s crew, so how exactly they contrived to get wounded Will Moffat and the bereft Black Jake Johnson through a tropical jungle and back to the beached vessel is beyond my ken. Young Will himself—after he regained something of his senses to find himself aboard the *Sea Witch*, with 'Mister' Billy Browen in command—could remember nothing of it, which should explain my own uncertainty.

"However, from then on the strangeness grew and grew. What strangeness? Why, the evil power of the golden garment from the sky, of course! By day, the mazed and often-babbling Black Jake—pale Jake now, and vacant eyed—stayed in a locked room just above the bilges; but by night . . . well, who can say? If he got out, and we must assume he did by reason of what occurred, then how? Perhaps someone let Jake out, but why? Or maybe that weird sky-stuff simply unwrapped itself to slip out on its own! Young Will couldn't even hazard a guess, and neither can I. But for a fact *some-*

thing got out—Jake or the golden garment, one or the other—and as for what occurred:

"At first they called it 'the scourge': a lethal strain of scurvy which they'd witnessed just once before, except now they had their doubts. And after four of the crew went down with it, night after night on four consecutive nights, then they considered their doubts confirmed. And aye, I have read it in your mind, Necroscope, that you have knowledge of this thing: from Billy Browen, no doubt? What, the scourge? A kind of scurvy? This shrivelling horror, that warped strong men to bags of bones, killing each one of them in a single night . . . ?

"But Billy Browen was alert now, watching how things went: seeing members of the crew sidling off—going down below decks one by one, somehow *lured* down there—to gaze in rapt fascination through knotholes and gapped boards at their once-Captain in his golden kirtle. Or maybe it wasn't so much Jake that they stared at as the sky-stuff.

"As for Billy himself:

"So far he'd done as his 'darlin' Cap'n' requested of him; he'd looked after both Black Jake and young Will when they were incapable of taking care of themselves. Now, however—despite that the gradually mending, occasionally lucid youth would show Billy his blackened, withered hands—'Mister' Browen found himself ever more frequently lured below decks, just like the rest of the crew, to stare at a glassy-eyed Black Jake in the coldly glittering glow of the thing he wore . . . or rather, to stare at the thing that wore Jake as once it had worn Zhadia. . . .

"Then one morning it was discovered that another four crew members, probably four of the strongest willed, had seen and so feared what was going on that they'd stolen a recently acquired rowboat and jumped ship; by which time the entire crew—or the handful that remained—had fallen into this dreadful malaise, no longer carrying out their rightful duties but forever sneaking belowdecks to look at the man in the golden robe.

"Which was how things stood when a naval warship, creeping

up on the *Sea Witch* one night, blew a hole in her hull right on the waterline and finished her off for good.

"Will Moffat, while he would never more be entirely whole, at least had certain of his wits about him that night; or so he told me. Enough that as the vessel began to settle in the water he followed Billy below to warn him against what he believed he was about to do. For Billy was now so mazed in his own mind, so enamoured of the sky-stuff, that he wasn't about to let it founder with the *Sea Witch*; while Will—for all that he was a mere lad—had resisted the sky-cloth's attraction for so long that he was now mainly immune to it. But still he knew what it could do to others . . . and Billy Browen was the only man in the world who had ever shown him anything of real friendship.

"And so as Billy came to Jake's cell, already knee-deep in water, young Will caught up with him. The two looked in on Jake standing there with a cocked pistol to his head; where he'd got the weapon, who could say? Stolen on one of his outings: it had to have been.

"Billy knocked the wedge from the door, yanked it open and reached for a corner of golden weave. Will rasped, 'Mister Browen, take care! *Leave it be!*' Black Jake cried, 'Mister, I'm all done in, so to hell with you and everybody else!' With which he squeezed his trigger, blew his ear off and a hole right through his head.

"Shocked into his right mind, and gibbering in his terror, Billy clambered up towards the tilting deck; but before he could get there the sky-thing came wafting after. Having left Jake it now wrapped Billy like a shroud, stunning him with the agony of transition.

"As for young Will Moffat: when he saw Billy stagger, stumble, and tumble overboard, he just lay down in the rising water and prayed for an easy death—

"—Which as it happened wasn't in his stars.

"Will and Billy—the only survivors of the old *Sea Witch*—they were plucked from the briny, thrown in the man-o'-war's brig, and were delivered to justice in Hartlepool when the ship got blown off course for London in a storm. Since both men were mazed and lacking finances they could neither defend themselves nor purchase a lawyer; and in any case they were pirates from a notorious ship, the sole survivors of Jake Johnson's *Sea Witch*, and there had been a price on Billy's head for almost a decade. All of these terms are Will Moffat's, of course, which I'm sure you will understand far better than I did.

"Anyway, to get done with this:

"They were hung high right here on the harbour wall, young Will in a metal jacket to keep bits from falling off and stinking in the nostrils of the people, but loose enough so the seagulls and crows could feast on him; Billy Browen in his 'cloth-of-gold' robe, probably because it scarred the hands of any who tried to relieve him of it. . . .

"And that's that, Necroscope: as much as Will Moffat remembered of his life up to the point where he and Billy Browen got strung up on the sea wall. But for all Will's time as a pirate, the lad's suffering must have counted in his favour; there must have been lots of goodness in him for the Valkyrie to carry him off so quickly, while me and mine have spent all these hundreds of years here.

"And now that really is it, I've said my lot. Except—

"—Maybe now you'll understand what so concerned me after I saw how you felt drawn back to that old graveyard. For that's where Billy Browen is to this day, Harry, and who's to say what cerecloths his old bones are wearing now, eh . . . ?"

Who indeed? thought the Necroscope.

And while the urgency within persisted, while yet he felt the need to return at once to the cemetery, Erik's final words, spoken in genuine concern, gave Harry sufficient pause that his movements were less than hurried when he got down from the harbour wall, stretched his legs to revitalise them, then leaned on the wall and stared out over the water. For some few minutes he stood there thinking things through, considering his position.

Events were more and more beginning to make sense, not all of it to his liking. If indeed there was danger in Hartlepool's old cemetery, surely the Great Majority would have known of it? And if they knew of it why hadn't they warned him? For they had had plenty of opportunity. Those of them lying at some distance from the graveyard might be innocent of knowledge, but the teeming dead who actually inhabited—no, bad word; "dwelled" then? No, even worse, for it implied life—who were *ensconced* there, they would certainly have known of any problem.

And what of that wall of deadspeak babble and interference which they had thrown up between the Necroscope and Erik Haroldson and the old graveyard itself? If they didn't want Harry and the Viking's conversation to be overheard, why not simply bring the danger—whatever it might prove to be—to Harry's attention, enabling him to raise his own shields and so preserve his privacy? Or was there perhaps something in that graveyard which they feared desperately, even more than they loved Harry Keogh? Well, possibly. But did that mean that he should fear it, too?

Oh yes, very definitely!

For the teeming dead, *being* dead and quite beyond harm—*apparently*—should have little or no reason to fear anything. Yet the Necroscope knew of things that even the Great Majority dreaded . . . no less than he himself: things he should avoid at all cost! Except *being* the Necroscope, he was the sworn guardian of the dead.

For which reason—

—He moved from the sea wall and sought cover, and hidden however briefly from human eyes conjured metaphysical maths and took the Möbius route back to the ancient graveyard. But now as he moved between the old plots, Harry was more than ever alert, taking in all that was available to his eyes, ears, and nostrils of the scenery, silence, and lurking imminence of the place. And its imminence was such that he could almost feel its weight—

—Until he realised that this weight he felt was actually a gradually building hum, a throb, the burgeoning din of energies that seemed to be issuing from . . . *from the Necroscope himself!* Harry was the psychic "dynamo," the human mechanism that was converting energy into the vibrant current that was emanating from him! But who or what was tapping into Harry's unique mind, feeding it alien energy and using it as an amplifier? To what weird receiver was this involuntary signal being transmitted, and what information was it carrying? A complete mystery: the Necroscope might hazard a reasonable guess in answer to at least one of these questions, the first of them, but he had no definite answer to any of them—not yet.

Flinching from a blinding migraine that came stabbing out of nowhere to parallel Harry's new concept and reduce his sensitivity to his surroundings, he approached Billy Browen's grave. But then, as he stumbled against a tombstone that marked one of several previously noted, partly sunken plots, the groping hand with which he steadied himself revealed a badly weathered skull and crossbones design in crumbling bas-relief. The names, dates, and epitaphs, long since faded and lichened over, were unreadable, but the engraving itself told its own story, however inarticulate.

Employed almost universally in times immemorial as death's principal indicant, this macabre sigil was also that of pirates and their trade. And now, as Harry looked more attentively from headstone to ivied headstone, he saw that the leaning, occasionally broken markers over *all* of these oddly concave graves bore the selfsame grisly motif. What was more, this handful of partially collapsed plots had been arranged about Billy Browen's in something of an irregular semicircle—almost as if to enclose it against the cemetery's rear wall. . . .

This meant something, Harry was sure. If not for the damnable buzzing and throbbing in his head, and the lights flashing before his eyes, he believed he might even be able to sense the revenants of the old pirates who were buried here holding their deadspeak breath! But while they appeared unwilling to speak to him, there remained at least one other "old pirate" who was:

Harry? Is it you? came the enquiry in a "voice" previously presumed to be deadspeak—except now Harry saw that it wasn't deadspeak but a perfect imitation, telepathy of a sort—and in no way a communication from a dead creature but from someone or thing very much alive, which yet issued from the grave to which he now felt irresistibly drawn. And:

Ah, but of course! the voice went on, boldly now and even mockingly, showing never a trace of its previous piratical parlance. *Of course it is the Necroscope, Harry Keogh himself! Who else could it be? Who else with a mind powerful enough to reach out to the stars and perhaps into other places? Who so dark and yet so innocent, fallible, that he can err, and grievously? Who of such enormous, misplaced conceit, that having confronted and defeated even the worst of men and monsters, he now believes he is invincible? A conceit which discovers nothing to fear in the allure of one who fell from the sky and was crippled. I am that one . . . ! Hurt, I gradually healed myself, conserving my energies down all the decades and even the centuries until the coming of a saviour—your coming, Harry!*

"Crippled? Healed yourself?" the Necroscope mumbled, clutching at his temples, going to his knees in the crumbly soil of Billy and something else's grave. And even knowing the danger now, still he felt drawn like an iron filing to a magnet, fascinated by something in the ground, hypnotised, almost paralysed by a power which—inasmuch as it could use him like this, in a manner and for a purpose as yet undisclosed—must be at least the equal of his own.

Yes I preserved myself, the sky-thing continued, *conserved my energies, healed myself with the lives and discarded* materia *of an alien species—your species, Harry—ever hoping against hope that a mind such as yours would one day stray within range of my allure. But when finally that time dawned I was still too weak to take advantage, too afraid of your strength to approach you. Having usurped the mind of Billy Browen, I heard you speak to others who were buried here; and while I waited, I strove to learn the language of my host, to speak with his voice and mannerisms. Not difficult: his mind was mine from which to draw all such knowledge! But while all of this was several years ago, the waiting was only over when finally I knew that I could best you . . . which was today, when you returned to me and I saw that you could not resist my allure.*

On his knees beside the blank marble marker, reeling like a drunkard from the pain in his head, the Necroscope was barely able to control his thoughts when he mouthed: "But who . . . *what* are you?"

A survivor! came the answer. *I survived a war out there in the stars. When my vessel was destroyed and I fell to earth, or rather into an ocean, the water sapped what little strength remained in me; your sun's rays revived me, returned something of my vitality, but not enough. The host creatures who succored me—on whom I relied for sustenance, the energies of their minds and bodies— had died with my ship; but I discovered an alternative subsistence in the men who rescued me from the sea . . . as I believe "Billy Browen" has already informed you. Oh, indeed!*

Reeling to alien laughter, Harry said, "First Zhadia, then Black Jake and the crew of . . . of the *Sea Witch* . . . and finally Billy. No, finally *me!*" He rocked this way and that, clutching his skull as the hammering in his brain grew unbearably louder. "And the fact is I've never even met . . . never met or spoken to . . . to the *real* Billy! But what . . . what is it you're doing . . . doing to me? And why . . . why are you doing it?"

As the Necroscope fought to stay upright where he kneeled, suddenly he felt the earth shift beneath him: just a tremor, or a groping in the darkness of the dirt, but it filled him with a name-less dread. He knew he should up and run, but the magnetism of the thing in Billy Browen's grave held him in place, and his mur-derous migraine continued to weaken him. It was all he could do to stay vertical against the alien attraction, while beneath his knees the soil was beginning to move like quicksand.

Down there the thing from the stars wormed laboriously for the surface, loosening dirt and pushing it aside as it strained upwards for the light. Its "voice" was also strained as it answered Harry's question:

Your mind has the power which mine has lost. Now that you are drawn to me I can inspire your mind to greater efforts yet: such efforts will kill you, of course . . . even now the pressure builds within your brain, and you will die to give me life. You must suffer a little while longer; but only a little while. For even now the signal our combined minds are sending to the stars is being answered . . . and I sense others of my kind on their way to rescue me.

Harry gasped, choked in his agony, and tried to do what he should have done at the first sign of trouble: conjure a Möbius door right there alongside him on the grave, and topple himself through it. But the metaphysical maths resisted him; instead of esoteric equations, fabulous formulae, the screen of the Necroscope's mind issued an invisible beam not only into the sky but into *all* space! It travelled, not at the speed of light but the speed of thought; in fact it did not "travel" at all but simply "became" instantaneously! And yes, certain others were speeding to its source, to planet Earth, to this graveyard and the alien star-being that was now emerging from Billy Browen's plot.

A tumult of other voices—but true deadspeak voices now, from myriad cemetery plots silent until now—sprang into sudden, urgent existence in the Necroscope's psychic perception:

Go now, Harry, leave! Now that we know what this thing is, and that it will soon depart, save yourself! Use your powers to put miles, leagues, the span of a world between, where the creature's will, its weird allure, can no longer reach you!

With what small part of his consciousness remained to him, Harry answered in their own mode: *And now you speak to me, when it's too . . . too late. What was I, then? Some kind of scapegoat or sacrifice? My Möbius numbers are gone, obscured in the energies that this thing is channelling through me! I can't . . . can't move!*

The graveyard was empty of all living souls save the Necroscope himself . . . no possibility of help from any human hand or agency, not of the corporeal variety. Beside Harry the soil was bulging; something mobile, dull, the colour of patinated bronze, was pushing aside the earth beneath the marble slab, causing it to tilt. The once-golden sky-thing, almost drained of energy no less than Harry—its allure beginning to wane, but yet strong enough to hold him in place, to fascinate him as it had fascinated

Zhadia and the crew of the *Sea Witch*—was exhuming itself into the daylight!

The edge of a sentient, liquid bronze blanket curled over, touched Harry's arm, froze for a split second . . . then quivered and stuck like glue! It immediately assumed a glowing lustre, a saffron sheen that moved rapidly from the point of contact down into the thing's bulk where it was still buried in the dirt.

The Necroscope cried out, lifted a shaking hand, and like the proverbial drowning man who clutches at straws, grasped the exposed rim of the marble slab and exerted leverage. It was his last, desperate attempt to push back from the lure of the star-thing.

The partly tilted marker toppled onto its back, revealing its underside. And through eyes that could barely see by reason of the migraine that was tormenting him, finally Harry was able to read the inscription—a badly engraved couplet, its crudely erratic, antique lettering all clogged with dirt—which until now had lain hidden, sight unseen:

Here lie the remains of Billy Browen—
Pray God this stone helps keep him down!

Harry's arm to the shoulder felt cold . . . and yet it was a very terrible cold that was beginning to burn. In parallel, the edge of liquid metal where it seemed to have fused with his arm had become a siphon, gleaming an even brighter golden hue as it grew stronger, leeching on the Necroscope's physical as opposed to his mental energies.

Again Harry cried out, not in protest at the numbing sensation in his arm and shoulder—though that was a cold-burning pain in itself—but by reason of the bomb bursts of fire that were melting his mind, the agonising brilliance of the migraine that was killing him.

And his cries were answered.

Dust spiralled up from burial plots all around, especially from a grave some small distance beyond the four marked with skull and crossbones symbols, whose headstones stood like sentinels in a roughly delineated semicircle around the place where Harry kneeled in dirt and leaf-mould. It was the dust of forgotten men— of men long dead! The dust of bones fretted by grave worms and acidic soil, ground down by time and set aside by the action of gravediggers at their grim duties. The dust of flesh perished beyond corruption, withered, desiccated, and sifted to the surface on cold, careless shovels. This whirling dust devil—suddenly sentient and full of purpose—rushed in upon Harry as if to smother him!

But the Necroscope wasn't its target.

The dirt in Billy Browen's grave erupted as the thing from the stars finally emerged in full. Its form seemed lightweight, almost as if it had no weight at all, as it rose above the plot and wafted into the air; and yet it took Harry with it, lifting him to his feet as his eyes grew dull and began to glaze over—

—Which was when the dust devil hit!

It slammed into, stuck, and layered itself upon the undulating star-thing, settling an inch thick on the billowing shape and causing it to whip, trying to dislodge the dust but shaking free the Necroscope instead. And now another ethereal deadspeak voice— a voice that Harry had never heard before—reached him through the general psychic uproar from every part of the graveyard. It came to him more clearly by reason of its source being close to hand: namely the plot which had first issued the dust, the lifeless organic *materia* of a once-man, now clinging to the panicking star-thing. Harry's unshielded thought processes with regard to what was happening were deadspeak, of course, and:

A once-man? the newcomer's spirit answered, all unbidden. *Aye, Necroscope—and a once-pirate, at that!*

Sprawling in the dirt, then backing away from the frantic star-thing on all fours, finally clambering to his feet, albeit unsteadily, to put a handful of staggering steps between, Harry shook some of the numbness and burning cold out of his hand and arm and mumbled: "Who are you? But never mind: whoever you are, you have my thanks!"

Thanks, too, to whatever force had severed the telepathic, hypnotic connection between him and the creature, relieving the incredible pressure on Harry's metaphysical mind, where already far fewer suns were bursting into novas. And before his unknown benefactor could reply, as Harry found himself once more capable of reasoned thought—and that with a greatly reduced amount of pain and effort—he hazarded a guess and answered his own question:

"You and these others here, surrounding Billy's grave: you are the ones who jumped ship in a rowboat, when the rest of the crew were surrendering to this thing's allure. You made arrangements to be buried here when life was done, perhaps thinking to use yourselves as a barrier between the world of living men and the evil intelligence of a parasitic being from the stars. Am I right?"

The being he referred to was moaning, groaning in his mind now. *Ohhhhh, Necroscooope! You seek to murder me, but too late. They come for me, out of the stars. I feel them close. And when they have taken me up— when I command a ship again—you and this world where I have languished for so long, you shall know such suffering, and I shall know satisfaction!*

The creature tried to float in Harry's direction; weighed down in dust, it flopped, floundered. Nothing of brightness was any longer visible; the clinging debris of long-dead men closed out the light and natural energy of the sun. The thing's colour in a handful of places where its convulsions dislodged clots of dust showed leaden grey in the brief moments before that unrelenting organic debris flew back and adhered once again.

And meanwhile the unknown ex-pirate was answering Harry's questions:

As to your first: who I am or was does not matter; I am no longer, except as one who waits for better things. Your second: the four who lay closest to Billy's grave—no longer here but long since moved on—were indeed the four who fled the ship in its final hours; each made his arrangements even as you surmise. Your third, however, that they came here to use themselves as a barrier to hem the thing in, is a noble thought incorrectly ascribed. We were pirates, Harry, who in the main cared not a jot for our so-called "fellow men!" The four were drawn here by the creature's allure: to the end of their days they still felt it, and when it was time they came here to die, just to be near it! Aye, and myself "in the same boat," as it were. But I had lived the longest and there was no space for a plot any closer to the vampire . . . to that evil, glorious golden sky-thing . . . !

"You admired it; you even desired it?" Still backing away from the star-creature, Harry shook his head in disbelief.

No more than you yourself, Harry. No, I didn't desire it—but I felt its power, its allure, even when far away from it. I had known it for too long a time: first when we rescued it from the sea, then aboard the Sea Witch, *finally in young Will Moffat's jungle bolt-hole, when the creature held Zhadia in thrall, using her body and wasting it.*

At last the Necroscope knew who he was. "You are the lone survivor of the six who deserted Black Jake during his search for Will Moffat after Will took Zhadia and ran off!"

Now you have me, the other replied, and Harry detected a loss of power in his deadspeak voice; also that it now seemed to come from an indeterminate location and gradually increasing distance. *First I deserted the* Sea Witch, *and then I fled from that devil Jake's onslaught on young Will's refuge. I was the lone survivor, aye, but I couldn't flee far enough . . . not from the golden thing's allure! Fortunately, as it grew weaker, my plot lay beyond its reach; yet even so, I would have wished to be closer! And now I see your next question, and once again you are correct: the thing reached out its siphons to the four who were buried closest—even to their dead bodies in all of their corruption—from which it has drawn sustenance down all these years!*

"The hollow plots!" Harry gasped, shocked despite that he had guessed correctly. And now there were other questions that he would ask, except:

Now I feel strange, said the other, his deadspeak failing, coming to Harry as from far away. *And I think: perhaps it is my time to move on! But thanks to you, at least I have touched the vampire thing: held it close, enveloped it, albeit in insensate dust. It even seems possible that where I am bound my soul will no longer hunger after it! I can only hope so. . . .*

With which his voice faded to nothing and he was gone.

Meanwhile the leaden grey thing had shaken itself free of

dust, and summoning the last of its alien energy it lunged for the Necroscope. Harry's Möbius math was intact; he conjured an invisible door—

—But he didn't put it to use. Once again frozen, held in stasis, the grip of a paralysing power, he swayed to and fro in the one spot, doing his level best to keep his balance. On this occasion, however, it wasn't the alien parasite that controlled him but others more powerful yet, and the thing itself was held immobile no less than Harry.

Then down from the dull sky came a beam no more vital than a ray of sunlight, but one that defeated gravity absolutely. Up went the once-golden thing, faster and faster into empty space, and Harry heard its dwindling shriek, the reason for which came almost at once as another telepathic voice announced itself:

Fear not for we mean you no harm. But we have searched for this evil one for long and long. He and his kind made war on us—indeed, on all of the universe's many races—and long since lost the battle. He is the last of his kind; all the others are restrained, contained. Like them he will be held in stasis with neither mental nor physical contact, lacking all forms of nourishment, until his energies devolve and his materia is consumed by the infinite void. We will not kill him, who can by no other means die, but let time perform the task for us.

As for you: a warning! Be mindful how you use your powers, which are great; use them only for the benefit of others, avoiding the inducements of all evil beings—such as this one—who may only seek to perform their grievous works through you!

Thus we counsel you. You are a chosen one, but immature as yet in the ways of the Higher Mind. And now farewell. . . .

And as the pale but powerful beam from above switched off, the Necroscope allowed his knees to bend and slid into a seated position with his back to a leaning headstone. . . .

Later, Harry conversed with the graveyard's spokesman:

"Why didn't you warn me? Your silence was deafening!"

We had ourselves been warned, said the spokesman. *Also, we didn't know what we were dealing with; or rather, what was dealing with us! We sus-pected some kind of vampire, but an eater of the dead as opposed to the living. And against vampires, Harry, well you have proved yourself invincible.*

Harry frowned. "You had yourselves been warned? By whom?"

By the creature itself! "Only speak of me to the Necroscope—" the star-thing told us, "—only alert him to his danger, and I shall send forth my siphons after you!"

Harry shook his head. "He was bluffing. He didn't have the strength."

We didn't know that, but we did know that you are *invincible!*

"No." Again Harry shook his head. "I'm not, and that thing very nearly proved it!"

For which . . . well, how can we say we're sorry? Obviously, sorry can never be enough. The spokesman was downcast, humbled; if he had eyes to cry, they would have.

But relenting, Harry disagreed with what the spokesman had said. "Because of all you have suffered, 'sorry' will more than suf-fice. Surely it's enough that you have left the world of the living behind and know only the bitter cold and the darkness of death in a crumbling box, without also being threatened there?"

Still, we were mistaken and we are sorry.

"No need." The Necroscope shook his head. He had spoken his last on the matter. . . .

He took the Möbius route to Hartlepool's ancient harbour, where he leaned on the weathered stone wall and looked out across the water. The sea was flat calm where, as the sky lightened, rafts of gulls floated in the sudden flash and sparkle of sunlight on the rip-ples, and the world felt fine indeed.

Harry said as much to anyone who would listen. Then, when no answer was forthcoming, he spoke directly to Erik "Scarhelm" Haroldson, to thank him for his warning—and again received no reply. But it wasn't that the Great Majority had soured on him. Not now, and not ever.

No, it was just that Erik was no longer here, neither him nor his Viking crew. Oh, their bones would be down there still, but as for their souls—

—Finally Erik had won them the right to move on.

To Valhalla? Well why not? Listening hard, the Necroscope even believed he heard the cries of the Valkyries. It was only the seagulls, but Harry pretended otherwise. . . .

End Piece: Old Man with a Blade

It was Edinburgh in the summer but could as easily be any city or place anywhere at any time, in any season since time began.

The old man with the blade, that long, curving ever sharp blade, was on the lookout, as usual, for fresh—or maybe not so fresh—victims. They had it coming eventually; but the way he looked at it they had done it and *were* doing it to themselves! Victims of their own stupidity . . . but in an equal number of cases victims of their genes; for as often as not, that was where it started.

Take for instance the old boy in the wheelchair pushed by his haggard-looking wife. A classic case of who would go first: him with his Alzheimer's—prompting him to stick his fingers in electric sockets, because he couldn't remember what they were—or her worn down by the weight of caring for him, whose problem

186

was in his genes, inherited from his father, who in turn had got it from *his* father . . . and so on. But both of them eventually, if not just yet.

The old man's curved blade tingled with a life of its own; its owner sensed it lusting after the lives of others—even of this harmless pair—but not yet. He leaned towards them anyway as they passed him by on the pavement, sniffing at them to make sure he wasn't mistaken. He wasn't, which in its way was disappointing; better them than some young couple. But then again it wasn't his lot to discriminate.

The street was as good as empty; on this early Sunday morning most folks were still abed or only just stirring. But there were, of course, those who were driven to be up and about. Like that middle-aged man who had just come out of the tobacconist's shop, already tearing the film from his pack of cigarettes, and then the silver foil, his hand trembling where it groped in his pocket for his lighter.

The old man with the shining blade stepped closer, smelled the smoke from that first long drag, heard the addict's sigh of relief . . . and also the cough welling up from the diseased lung of which, for the moment, the smoker wasn't aware. But he would be, oh he would be! As the curved blade tingled again, a little more determinedly now, the old man nodded to himself, thinking, "We'll give him a year, my faithful friend, or perhaps a little less." And he patted the long handle of his blade.

A little farther down the street, a bearded derelict wrapped in a torn blanket mumbled to himself where he lay in a shop doorway. Sucking the last few drops of wine from a brown bottle in a paper bag, he flopped back into a shady corner and waved a fluttery greeting to no one in particular. Grey vomit had hardened to crusts on his blue-veined naked feet.

"Ah!" said the old man with the tingling, sentient-seeming blade, also to no one in particular. And lifting the blade from the leather saddle on his shoulder, he reached into the doorway and touched the derelict's dirty neck. With his eyes closed and flesh numb, the bum saw and felt nothing at all . . . but then he wouldn't have anyway. And:

"Next winter," said the old man as he strode on along the street. "We'll see you again next winter."

Disease, drugs, drink, and occasionally accidents. And the absolute harvest of war, naturally. And always the old man with his shining blade: always Death, of course. He moved on.

The city was beginning to come awake now, daylight brightening. The old man wasn't especially fond of daylight: he suffered it but it didn't really fit the image of one who preferred to have things happen in the dark of night. However—and once again—it wasn't in his power to discriminate. . . .

There was a fancy wine bar with an ornate varnished mahogany facade, opaque, small-paned bull's-eye windows, and a hanging sign above the recessed, arched-over double doors that read simply: "B.J.'s." As the old man with the blade drew level with the doors they opened; a girl, beautiful, darkly gypsyish, with eyes that shone in the shaded doorway, ushered a young man into the daylight. She leaned forward to kiss him, a temporary farewell, left him on the street and closed the doors on him.

There was something about the young man. He blinked in the morning sunlight and lifted a hand to shade his pale face, his eyes that seemed a little distant, dazed and disorientated. The old man thought it possible that he knew that look: he believed he'd seen its like before: often, on the faces of men who were lost or bent on suicide!

And yet . . . there was something else about this particular young man, so the old man with the scythe leaned closer, sniffing out the other's origins, essence, nature, destiny. But then a singular thing: just for a moment he thought he saw the young man's faraway eyes focus and look back at him! And more, it was as if the young man knew him, as if they were old friends! .

Indeed they *were* old friends!

The scythe no longer tingled but shivered, and its master, the oldest man of all, shivered with it and jerked away, quickening his silent steps along the still mainly empty street. Ah, he knew this one now, remembered him for all the work he'd done for him; knew also that he would never be required to accommodate him. Oh, his time would come eventually—well, possibly—but not now and not in this world. That was not this one's destiny. But there were other old men with blades, a great many of them, in all the many worlds where life had taken root.

One of them would accommodate this one—this Necroscope, this Harry Keogh—well, eventually. Or possibly? Death stroked his living scythe to calm it, then paused to cast a glance back along the almost empty street. And then he nodded to himself.

For apart from a small dust devil where it collapsed close to the wine bar's entrance, and the dirty naked foot protruding from a shop doorway, the street *was* empty, yes.

And the old, old man moved on. . . .